She almost dropped the flask when a shadow fell across her

At the same second, she heard Sophie cry ecstatically "Daddy!" When she looked up, Gabriel was there, observing her gravely for an incredible moment, until Sophie flung herself into his arms. And as Josh followed suit, Gabriel held them both close and Laura saw the wetness of tears on his cheeks.

When the children had calmed down after lots of hugs and kisses and were tucking into the food, she asked in a low voice, "So you decided to come earlier?"

"Yes, but I'm not staying."

"The children won't like that! Don't you think they've waited long enough to be with you?"

"Yes, I do, but, Laura, my life has been on hold for long enough. I have things to sort out at the hospital. I want the way ahead to be clear with regard to my career, so that I know where I'm at, what I'm doing."

The hurt inside her was beyond bearing as she listened to what he was saying and it came forth in anger as she said tightly, "So nothing changes, Gabriel? It's still career first, and family second," she said, and with her glance on the children who were out of earshot, "Well don't let us stop you...."

Dear Reader,

Once again we meet between the pages of one of my books. This time it is the third story out of four about The Doctors of Swallowbrook Farm, and here we meet Gabriel, a doctor who has a great sense of dedication toward his profession, and Laura, his wife, who throws their lives into chaos quite unintentionally.

Their story is about the love and loyalty that binds them together at a time of great unrest in their lives, and how the strength of it finally brings back the happiness that they thought they had lost. I do hope that you will enjoy meeting them.

With very best regards,

Abigail Gordon

MARRIAGE MIRACLE IN SWALLOWBROOK

Abigail Gordon

TORONTO NEW YORK LONDON
AMSTERDAM PARIS SYDNEY HAMBURG
STOCKHOLM ATHENS TOKYO MILAN MADRID
PRAGUE WARSAW BUDAPEST AUCKLAND

Recycling programs
for this product may
not exist in your area.

ISBN-13: 978-0-373-06838-8

MARRIAGE MIRACLE IN SWALLOWBROOK

First North American Publication 2012

For Stephen and Judith who generously gave me their time and their hospitality while showing me Lakeland.

CHAPTER ONE

A SUMMER sun was shining when Laura Armitage drew back the curtains in the master bedroom of the house that her uncle had given her. Its mellow golden rays were spreading far and wide from the ripening corn in distant fields to the shores of the tree-lined lakeside nearby, but to the woman at the window the brightness of the morning was blotted out by dark uncertainties about the future.

A month ago she and her children had moved into a spacious old house that she'd had renovated in the beautiful lakeland village of Swallowbrook. She'd been offered the position of practice manager at the medical centre in the village and, desperate to leave London, she'd accepted the opportunity to take up where her uncle, who had held the position before her, had left off. He had gone to spend his retirement in Spain and as a parting gift had given her his house.

The children, eight-year-old Sophie and six-year-old Josh, loved the place after the noise and bustle of London. The lake, beautiful in all weathers, was encircled by a bracelet of rugged fells that attracted walkers and climbers from far and wide all the year round, especially at this time, while down below them an assortment of craft of all types and sizes sailed the lake's clear waters.

The children's favourite pastime was when the three of them sailed to its far reaches on one of the pleasure launches that went to and fro all the time during the hours of daylight. But wherever they went, whatever they did, there was always the same question coming from Sophie, 'Mummy, when is Daddy coming home?'

'Soon,' she would tell her gently. 'He is just so busy looking after the sick people.'

As she gazed unseeingly out of the window Laura thought that she would love Swallowbrook as much as they did if only Gabriel was there with them. Without him life had no meaning. But a horrendous turn of events had taken him from them and until he surfaced again she had no idea if the light of a marriage that had already begun to fade had been extinguished completely.

He knew that she'd taken her uncle up on his offer of the house called Swallows Barn, and that she was now employed at the practice from nine o'clock in the morning to when the children came out of the village school in the afternoon.

When she'd told him about her uncle's generosity he'd been less than enthusiastic, 'Fine, if that's what you want, Laura, but when I get out of here I intend to go straight to the town house.' And with a bleak smile he'd added, 'I take it that it's still there? That it hasn't been repossessed?'

'No. of course not!' she'd said steadily, holding back the tears that she had never shed in front of him on the nightmarish visiting days when they'd sat across from each other at a small table without touching and behaving like strangers.

She'd never wept in front of the children either, determined that nothing should spoil their youthful innocence. Her tears were shed in the long hours of the night in the big double bed that was bereft of the presence of the husband she'd adored.

'I've taken the job in Swallowbrook to help pay the bills while you're not around,' she'd told him that day. 'The gift of my uncle's house clinched it with regard to moving there, but from what you've just said it would seem that you aren't intending to join us. I thought you were desperate to see the children, Gabriel, knowing how much it must have cost you to refuse to let me bring them with me on days like today.'

'I *am* desperate,' he'd said grimly, 'but first I want to get a decent haircut, and to be able to turn up looking the same as when they last saw me. Yet it doesn't mean that every day I'm without them isn't hell on earth.'

'And what is every day without *me* like?' she'd asked, stung by the lack of any mention of herself.

'An exercise in accepting that I was never

there when you needed me, and in the end for a fleeting moment I mistakenly thought you'd turned to someone else,' he'd said in the same flat tone.

'Yes, and when you came home early for once and found me in another man's arms, you felt entitled to become judge and jury without providing the opportunity for any explanation, *and* nearly killed someone who *did* want my company,' she'd parried, without raising her voice in the crowded visitors' area.

They'd gone over the same ground countless times while they'd been waiting for the court hearing, and it was only the fact that he had resuscitated and brought back to life the man he had attacked when he'd found him holding her close that had saved Gabriel from a longer sentence than the one he was serving now.

He had dragged her free of his hold and with one fierce blow had sent Jeremy Saunders reeling backwards and his head had hit the big marble fireplace behind him with an ominous crack. When they'd bent over him they'd discovered that his heart had stopped beating and it had been then that Gabriel had come to his senses and his medical training had kicked in.

She turned away from the window and slowly made her way downstairs, the hurt of that conversation as raw as ever, and saw that it was time to look forward instead of back if the children were to get to school on time.

They had settled into life in the country as to the manner born, with Sophie her usual caring self where her small brother was concerned. She was like Gabriel in both looks and personality, dark hair, hazel eyes, quick thinking and determined when it came to life choices, even at such an early age.

Josh was more like her, or rather how she used to be. She was no longer steadfast and tranquil, wrapped around with the contentment of the joys that life had brought her in the form of a husband she adored and who adored her in return, and a small son and daughter to cherish.

They'd lived in one of London's tree-lined

squares, not far from where Gabriel had practised as a consultant oncologist working entirely within the NHS and very much in demand, so much so that over the last few years she had begun to feel like a one-parent family because he was never there.

Both of his parents had died of cancer when he'd been in his teens and on choosing medicine as a career he had decided to specialise in oncology. Every life he was instrumental in saving from the dreadful disease helped to make up a little for the loss of those he had loved.

She had always known and accepted that was the reason for his dedication to his calling, but as time had gone by the ritual of him arriving home totally exhausted in the early hours of the morning and being asleep within seconds of slumping down beside her on the bed that was so often empty of his presence had begun to tell.

Then it would be back to the hospital again almost before it was daylight and their physical relationship had become almost non-existent as it had seemed that his obsession with his career was going to drive them apart if he didn't ease off a little to give them some time to be a family.

It had been of all things a swelling in her armpit that had brought everything to a climax. Gabriel had already left the house and been on his way to the hospital one morning when she'd been drying herself after coming out of the shower and had felt something under her arm that hadn't been there before.

Immediately concerned, she'd phoned him to tell him about it and on the point of performing a major operation on a cancer patient he'd said, 'Pop along to the surgery and get them to have a look at it, Laura. I'm just about to go into Theatre.'

She'd put the phone down slowly. No woman on earth would want to find a lump in the place she'd described, but she was the lucky one, or so she'd thought. Her husband was one of the top names in cancer treatment, so it was to be expected that anything of that nature with regard to his wife would have his full attention, *but instead he'd told her to see her GP who, knowing who her husband was, had observed her in some surprise.*

He had tactfully made no comment and after examining the swelling had told her, 'It could be anything, Mrs Armitage, but we doctors never take any chances with this sort of thing, so I will make you an appointment to see an oncologist. Have you any preferences?'

'Er, yes, my husband,' she'd told him, and his surprise had increased, but it hadn't prevented the appointment being made for the following day.

When she'd arrived at the hospital Laura had seated herself in the waiting room with the rest of those waiting to be seen and when a nurse had appeared and called her name she had followed her into the room where Gabriel was seeing his patients.

He'd been seated at the desk with head bent, having been about to read the notes that he'd just taken from the top of the pile to acquaint himself with the medical history of his next patient. When he'd looked up she'd watched his jaw go slack and dark brows begin to rise as he'd asked, 'What are *you* doing here, Laura? Can't you see that I'm busy?'

'I need to see you,' she'd said implacably.

'Whatever it is, surely this is not the right place to discuss it,' he'd protested. 'Can't you wait until I come home?'

'No, I can't, that's why I'm here, Gabriel. You're never there, and it isn't anything domestic I want to discuss. I'm here as a patient.'

'What!' he'd exclaimed. 'Why? What's wrong with…?' His voice had trailed into silence as for once his quicksilver mind hadn't been working at top speed, and then realisation had come. 'The swelling in your armpit? You've been to see the GP?'

'Yes,' she'd told him woodenly. 'He managed to conceal his surprise at me consulting him when I'm married to one of the country's leading oncologists and made me an appointment. I'm surprised that my name didn't register with your secretary, but she wouldn't be expecting me here as a patient, I suppose.'

'Let me see it,' he'd said as remorse washed over him in shock waves, and as he'd felt around the swelling they were both acutely aware that it was the first time he'd touched her in months and it had to be for something like this.

'It's difficult to say,' he'd announced as she'd replaced the top that she'd taken off. 'It could be hormonal, or muscular strain, even a benign tumour, so don't let's jump to any conclusions until we've done the necessary tests, which I'll set up for tomorrow. Okay?'

'Yes,' she'd said, and without further comment was about to depart.

'If you will hang on for a few moments, I'll run you home,' he'd offered contritely, but she'd shaken her head.

'No, thanks. I'll be fine.' And before he could protest, she'd gone.

Amongst the uncertainties of her life, the position that Laura had taken up in the medical practice at Swallowbrook was like a calm oasis in spite of the pressures of a busy surgery and enough paperwork to keep her fully occupied.

There were four doctors in the practice, husband and wife Nathan and Libby Gallagher, and Hugo Lawrence, newly married to Ruby Hollister, who had joined them some months previously as a junior doctor. But soon they would be down to three again as Libby was pregnant and about to become a full-time mother to her new baby and Toby, their six-year-old adopted son. Laura had been working in hospital administration when she'd met Gabriel Armitage and the attraction between the clever oncologist who had a dark attractiveness that made him stand out amongst other men, and the serene golden haired vision behind a desk in the office had been an instant thing.

It had been at the hospital's Christmas ball they'd met and the romance had progressed from there with wedding bells not long after, and until Gabriel had become one of the area's leading experts on cancer and in huge demand, they had been a united happy family with their two children.

But the end of that had come on the day when he had arrived home early for once and along with his anguished regret for letting a situation develop where his wife had been forced to make an appointment to see him, he'd brought flowers, a huge bouquet made up of all the blooms she loved the most.

But no one on the staff at the surgery knew much about her, and for the moment she was happy to keep things that way. As far as they were concerned, she had taken up the job on Gordon Jessup's recommendation.

Though she'd carefully kept details of her private life to herself it seemed as if her new colleagues assumed that her marriage had suffered a split, and it was altogether easier to let them continue to think this, at least until she had some idea herself of where things were going with Gabriel.

Still, her new workmates had been very welcoming. The two Gallagher doctors had invited Laura and the children round for afternoon tea one Sunday as a welcoming gesture and Toby and Josh, of a similar age, had hit it off immediately, while Sophie, who was the proud owner of a pink mobile phone, had received a call and chatted non-stop to the caller on a bench in the garden while the boys kicked a ball around close by.

'That was Daddy,' she'd said with cheeks flushed and eyes sparkling as they'd walked home, unaware of her mother's heartache because Gabriel hadn't had anything to say to her. How could they ever hope to mend their marriage if Gabriel wasn't even prepared to talk to her? Or for him was it simply too late? Did he want out of the marriage once he got out of prison?

They'd gone in the ambulance to A and E on that dreadful day, with Gabriel and paramedics watching over Jeremy Saunders, and she huddled beside them in a state of shock brought on by what had happened to him and the knowledge that Gabriel, who had been her joy and her life no matter how much he was absent from it, had thought her capable of infidelity.

If he'd arrived just a few seconds later he would have seen her pushing the other man away and sending him packing, but after what had happened earlier in the day he'd been in no state for coherent thought after his wife had come to see him as a patient who might or might not have cancer *because she hadn't been able to get his attention any other way.*

The police had been waiting at the hospital when they'd got there, having been notified by the ambulance crew of the circumstances of the emergency they were bringing in, and while the injured man was being treated Gabriel had been arrested on suspicion of grievous bodily harm.

She would have gone to the police station with him but he had insisted that she stay with their neighbour, who lived alone and as far as they knew had no close relatives, and there had also been the matter of their children due out of school soon.

'Phone the school, Laura,' he'd instructed, as, still in shock, she had stood by white faced and trembling. 'Ask them to keep the children there until you can pick them up.' As he'd been led away she'd nodded mutely and done as he'd said.

In the early evening, with Gabriel still at the police station, his secretary had phoned to say that his solicitor had been on the phone with a message from his client to say that her husband was insisting that she keep the appointments that had been made for her the following day and that he would be back as soon as possible.

'Whatever is wrong, Mrs Armitage?' Jenny Carstairs had asked, mystified at the unusual turn of events.

'It is something that we got involved in this afternoon, Jenny,' she'd told her, 'and knowing how Gabriel likes to have all ends neatly tied he's sending me a reminder about the scans, that's all.'

As soon as the secretary had gone off the line she'd rung the hospital to check on Jeremy's condition, knowing that if it had been someone other than Gabriel who had struck him he might not have survived the terrific blow to the head on the marble fireplace.

Jeremy was responding to treatment, she'd been told, there was no bleeding inside the head but he had sustained a skull fracture that was being dealt with, and his heart was being monitored all the time.

So it had seemed that Gabriel's quick response to what he'd been responsible for had probably saved the other man's life and she'd had to be satisfied with that, knowing

that her husband was in police custody because of his angry reaction at finding her
in the arms of another man.

Jeremy had seen her arrive home in tears
and had been quick to step in to offer the
comfort of his arms to his attractive neighbour in her moment of weakness. He'd been
holding her close and stroking her hair, and
at the moment that Gabriel had arrived he
had been taking advantage of the situation
and kissing her, and Gabriel had misunder-
stood what was happening.

As he put his key in the lock of the London
house, the feeling of unreality that had been
there all the time he'd been serving his sentence didn't lift. He was free of the punishment he'd received for loving his wife too
much, he thought grimly, but what now?
He looked around a hall that smelt musty
from the lack of fresh air, and as he opened
a window wondered if maybe that was how
he smelt, *for the same reason.*

Would Laura ever forgive him for doubt-
ing her? She'd visited him dutifully while
he'd been in that place but every time he'd

seen her he'd known that the bonds that had always held them together had been broken and it had been due to his neglect.

After her appointment as a patient on that never-to-be-forgotten day almost a year ago, he'd sat staring into space as the reality of what was happening to their marriage had hit him. The woman he loved had been reduced to consulting him as a member of the general public. They'd lived in the same house, slept in the same bed, yet that was what she'd had to do to bring his attention to something that could have been serious.

Laura hadn't known at that moment that he'd passed all his appointments for the day to his second in command when she'd left and in the early afternoon had gone home with the intention of telling her that in future his dedication to the sick and suffering wasn't going to take over his life as much as it had been doing, that they were going to be a proper family again.

With that in mind he had arrived to find her being kissed and cuddled by the guy who lived next door, who was the laziest devil he'd ever come across and considered himself to be irresistible to women. Of independent means, he spent his days socialising with the city 'jet set' while he, Gabriel, was often operating for twenty-four hours non-stop, and in those first few seconds of rage it had seemed to him as if the sloth from next door had turned his attentions to Laura.

When his case had come up in court he'd been sentenced to nine months in prison for grievous bodily harm and been told it would have been twelve if it hadn't been for the fact that as well as endangering the other man's life he had also saved it in those first few moments of realising the horror of what he'd done, otherwise he might have been facing a charge of manslaughter. The marble fireplace had played its part, but he had been the one who'd struck the blow and his life and Laura's had never been the same since.

In the weeks prior to his case coming up they had slept in separate rooms, discussed only household matters and the children's welfare, and though he was no weakling mentally or physically the thought of being shut away from her and the children for any length of time had been agony. The only bright spot had been that Laura's test results had come back negative for cancer. The swelling was benign.

The first thing he did in the silent house was strip off and wash away the smell of where he'd been, and then got dressed in some of his own casual clothes that had hung unworn over the months.

When he opened the fridge it was well stocked and he wondered when Laura had found time to drive up to London to do that. He had the answer when a few seconds later the phone rang and Jenny, his secretary, was on the line, welcoming him home and asking if the food she'd bought him was all right.

'Laura rang and asked me to do a shop for you,' she explained.

'It is fine, Jenny,' he told her, 'and many thanks for taking the trouble'

'It was no trouble. I'm just glad to know you're home,' she said awkwardly. 'Everyone on the unit wants to know when you're coming back.'

'It might be if rather than when,' he replied. 'I've got some thinking to do, Jenny, but I'll be around to see you all soon.'

He finished his conversation with Jenny, but almost immediately the phone rang again. This time it was Laura.

'Gabriel! You're home! Thank goodness! How does it feel?'

'Quiet, peaceful,' he replied. 'Jenny has done what you asked so I'm going to have a snack lunch and then maybe a walk in the park. I see that next door is up for sale. Did you know?'

'Er, yes. Jeremy phoned to tell me.'

'Why would he do that, then?'

'I don't know. I wasn't interested and told him so,' she said levelly, and into the silence that followed added, 'When are you coming to see the children?'

'Soon,' he replied. 'One day during the week maybe.'

'I see,' she replied, and she did. She saw that Gabriel had no intention of taking up where they'd left off on that dreadful afternoon. They'd lived like strangers in the same house after the event while waiting for the case to come up, and she was no more eager than he was to go back to that kind of life.

The move to Swallowbrook hadn't just been because of her uncle's generous gift of the house. She'd harboured a secret hope that it might be a new beginning with Gabriel away from the happenings of the past in a beautiful place, but it seemed that he had other ideas and when they'd finished the call she wept for all that they'd lost.

Laura had chaired a meeting of the doctors the night before to discuss a project that was already under way—the building of a clinic for cancer patients that Nathan Gallagher was keen to see take place on the same plot of land as the surgery.

The relevant authorities in the area had approved it and work had already started. The practice building had once been a farmhouse where Libby, his wife, had been brought up, and there was land to spare all around it.

The intention was that the clinic should be an offshoot of the local hospital's on-

cology department, which was always extremely busy, and if plans went ahead it would be somewhere for local people to see a consultant without a longer wait than was necessary.

Libby hadn't been at the meeting. She was retiring from the practice very soon and had suggested that Laura take Sophie and Josh round to their place to play with Toby until it was over.

When she'd dropped them off Libby had thought that the new practice manager looked tired and stressed but hadn't said anything, as on getting to know her better she was realising that Laura Armitage was a very private person.

The other woman in the practice, Hugo Lawrence's delightful new wife Ruby, who had joined them as a junior doctor some time ago, had similar feelings about the new practice manager and was doing her best to make her feel at home. She felt that Laura was under pressure of some kind and it was noticeable that there was never any mention of the children's father in any conversation with her.

Though not so with her young daughter, Sophie was obviously in touch with her father, even if her mother wasn't, if the number of times she mentioned him was anything to go by.

After speaking to Gabriel on Friday morning, Laura decided that if life had felt unreal ever since he'd come charging in and found the opportunist from next door using her distress to get to know her better, the stilted conversation they'd just had on the phone took unreality into a new dimension.

He still believed she'd been about to cheat on him, she thought. That she'd turned to Jeremy Saunders of all people because of his own neglect of her, and that maybe it hadn't been the first time. Never having been prepared to discuss it with her since, now he was making it clear that there wasn't going to be any loving reunion, not as far as he was concerned anyway.

Sleep was long in coming when she went to bed. As she lay wide-eyed beneath the eaves of Swallows Barn, Laura heard Sophie call out his name on a sob and couldn't

believe that Gabriel could stay away from the children now that he was free. If he didn't want to be with her, fine, but he adored Sophie and Josh, and if he didn't appear for them soon she would... What? *File for divorce and have to live without him for evermore?*

CHAPTER TWO

ON THE Sunday after Gabriel's release from prison, Laura set off with the children for a picnic on an island in the middle of the lake. It was a quiet and peaceful place, uninhabited except for just one property—an attractive house built from lakeland stone and appropriately named Greystone House.

They had told her at the surgery that it belonged to Libby and Nathan Gallagher, that he had bought it for her as a wedding present, and she'd thought how romantic that was. It seemed that the two of them and their small son spent every weekend there.

This Sunday the two doctors were going to the wedding of a friend who lived down south and so there would be no one but her and the children on the island today.

Sophie and Josh were keen to explore everywhere and as it was small enough for her to keep them in view all the time, she was happy to let them wander where they wanted as long as they didn't trespass on land belonging to the house.

Once they were happily occupied she set out the picnic for when they would be ready to eat, and then opening up the folding chair that she had brought with her settled herself on it and let her thoughts take over.

It hurt that Gabriel hadn't rushed straight up here to see the children at least, though he obviously had no interest in rebuilding their marriage.

She often thought that if she hadn't gone to the hospital as his patient that day, he wouldn't have come home so early, and when Jeremy had taken advantage of her distress, she would have sent him packing without Gabriel knowing anything about it and it would have been the end of the incident.

But Gabriel's timing had been all wrong and so had Jeremy's for that matter. They had all paid a high price for what had happened in the moment when his self-control had snapped. She could hear the engines of another passenger launch approaching and she sighed. It had stopped, and the peace she craved would be gone if others had the same thought in mind that she'd had.

Calling Sophie and Josh to her, she began to pour the cold drinks that she'd brought and almost dropped the flask when a shadow fell across her and the children came to a halt as if they'd seen a ghost.

She turned slowly with a tingling down her spine and when she looked up Gabriel was there, observing her gravely, and it was as if the four of them had been turned to stone, until Sophie broke the silence by crying 'Daddy!' and began running towards him, with Josh not far behind. As he scooped them up into his arms Laura saw the wetness of tears on his cheeks and thought achingly that this was a moment that none of them should ever have had to endure, but it had been thrust upon them. Where did they go from here?

Desperate to get away from the place where her life had been shattered, she'd spent the time that Gabriel had been away from her and the children picking up the pieces by moving to a new home in a beautiful Lakeland paradise, and although it had only been half a life without him there, she'd coped and would continue to do so whatever the outcome of his coming back to them.

When the children had calmed down after lots of hugs and kisses and were tucking into the food, she asked in a low voice, 'How did you know where to find us?'

'I didn't. I was parking the car by the lakeside when I saw the three of you in the distance boarding one of the launches, but it had sailed by the time I got there. I asked the girl in the ticket office if she knew where you were bound for. She said the island, so I caught the next boat.'

'I see. So you decided to come earlier?'

'Yes, but I'm not staying.'

'Oh, fine!' she said coolly. 'The children won't like *that*! Don't you think they've waited long enough to be with you?'

'Yes, I do, but, Laura, my life has been on hold for long enough. I have things to sort out at the hospital, matters that have accumulated while I've been in prison. I

want the way ahead to be clear with regard
to my career, so that I know my position,
what I'm doing.'

The hurt inside her was beyond bearing
as she listened to what he was saying and
it came forth in anger as she said tightly,
'So nothing changes Gabriel? It's still career first and family second.' She glanced
at the children, who were out of earshot.
'Well, don't let us stop you. Do dash off to
wherever it is you prefer to be.'

'Would it be all right to stay the night?'
he asked, with no answer forthcoming to
her protest.

'You shouldn't need to ask!'

The vestige of a smile was tugging at the
corners of the mouth that had kissed her
a thousand times in what seemed like another life.

'All right, then,' he said, adding with
grim humour, 'Just as long as the sheets are
of Egyptian cotton. My bedding of recent
months has hardly been luxurious, and if the
house has a spare room, that will do fine'

She turned away. How could he joke
about something like that and at the same

time make it clear that he didn't want to sleep with her? With a change of subject she pointed to the food and said stiffly, 'There is plenty to eat. What would you like to drink?'

As he squatted down on the grass, with the children chattering one on either side, it seemed so normal that she could hardly believe that for what had seemed like for ever the only man she had ever loved had been serving a custodial sentence for grievous bodily harm because of what had been the worst day of her life.

'I hope you'll like the house,' she said uncomfortably when they arrived at Swallows Barn with the children still on a high, having been driven home in Gabriel's car.

'If *you* are happy with it, that is all that matters,' he said levelly.

Sophie urged, 'Come and see my room, Daddy!'

'And mine!' Josh said, and as the three of them went upstairs together Laura thought that Gabriel could tell the children that he wasn't staying. She wasn't going to be re-sponsible for causing them any upset.

When they were asleep after receiving a promise from their father that he would take them to school the next morning, an awkward silence fell upon the house until it was broken by Gabriel asking casually, 'So what is the medical centre like in this place, Laura?'

Was that all he could talk about, health care? But she answered civilly enough, ex-plaining who was who and outlining her responsibilities.

They'd passed the practice on the way home and he'd noticed that a new building was being erected on the large plot of land next to it and had wanted to know what it was going to be.

'It is going to be a clinic that will be an offshoot of the main oncology unit at the local hospital,' she told him. 'All the staff at the surgery are very excited about it.'

'Hmm, impressive forward thinking,' he commented. 'When is it due to open?'

'Some time in the autumn if all goes according to plan.'

But she had questions of her own to ask and they weren't about health care. It was the first time she'd had the opportunity to ask him what it had been like being shut away from his life's work at the hospital and his family, and was hoping that his reply would give her some degree of understanding of the stranger that he had become.

'So what was it like in there?' she asked gently, and watched his face close up.

'It was a piece of cake.'

'I'm not asking for mockery,' she told him. 'I want the truth.'

It had been hell on earth being away from them, but he had brought it on himself. He must have been insane to think that Laura would have anything to do with the low life from next door, but seeing that creep with his arms around her had ignited a fury like he'd never known. Perhaps in hindsight his uncharacteristic behaviour had been amplified by his feelings of guilt over neglecting Laura.

He'd flung himself at the man like a

coiled spring and since that moment life had been totally unreal, but Laura was waiting for an answer and so, referring to the lighter side of his sentence, he said, 'I worked in the prison hospital for most of the time, which provided some degree of job satisfaction, and had a constant stream of inmates queuing up outside my cell for advice regarding their health problems, true or imaginary, but the nights were long.'

How long he couldn't bear to tell her, with visions of her coping with the children on her own, and in the middle of it all moving house, which showed clearly that by the time he was released she wanted to have made a new life for herself.

There *had* been indications that Laura wanted him to join her and the children in their new home, but he didn't want to rush into anything. Things had been going wrong between them even before that terrible incident. There was no way he could sidle back into her life without having something to offer in the form of trust and understanding, and the reason for him returning

to London the following day was connected
with that.

'And the rest of it?' she persisted.

'Not good in parts, but I had a debt to
repay, didn't I, Laura? And now I can get on
with my life knowing that ghastly episode is
over, that Saunders is fully recovered, and
that you and the children are all right.'

'And that is it?'

No, it isn't, he wanted to tell her. *When
you came to see me as a patient I had to accept that I wasn't being fair to you. That I
was guilty of gross neglect, and shortly afterwards I found myself believing that you
were betraying me with that guy of all people, that you'd turned to him for comfort. I
should have known better, of course, but I
wasn't thinking straight at the time.*

Instead he said, 'For the present, yes. I'll
keep in touch of course and if you need
me for anything don't be afraid to ask.' He
looked around him. 'Though you seem to
be managing very well without me.

'I sussed out the spare room while I was
upstairs, so will get my case out of the car

and settle down for the night if that's all right with you.'

'Don't you want a meal first?' she asked woodenly, bringing her mind back to basics, and when he shook his head a deadly calm began to settle upon her as the impact of his 'don't be afraid to ask' comment took hold.

In a measured tone she said, 'Just a moment before you go. You said if there is anything I need from you I have only to ask?'

He was observing her questioningly. 'Yes, I did. So is there something?'

'Yes. I want a divorce.'

She watched his jaw drop and amazement darken the hazel eyes looking into hers, and then he said in a grating voice that was nothing like his usual upbeat tone, 'So I was wrong. Am I still going to be paying for what I did?'

'And you think *I'm* not?' she said, doing her best to keep all emotion out of her voice. She could be just as coldly analytical as Gabriel if that was how he wanted things. 'I wanted you home, but not on the terms you're laying down in such a patronising manner. I've been living for the day when you were free of that place. But it seems that while you've had time on your hands you've been making plans that don't include me, which makes me think that you still aren't sure about how you found me in somebody else's arms, so, yes, Gabriel, I want a divorce!'

The strong lines of his face were set like granite as he turned and went out to the car without any further comment and when he came back inside she said, 'Breakfast will be ready at eight o'clock and if you still intend taking the children to school, they have to be there for quarter to nine.'

'Of course I'm going to take them,' he said levelly. 'I've never let *them* down!' *Like I have you,* the voice of conscience said.

Gabriel couldn't sleep. Twice he padded quietly to where the children were sleeping and gazed down on them tenderly, but the door of the master bedroom across the landing remained firmly shut. He had made everything worse between Laura and himself by not telling her what was in his mind. But first he had to speak to his friend James

Lockyer, chairman of the board of governors at the hospital where he'd worked.

Jenny kept phoning to say how much they were all looking forward to his return, but she had no say in the matter, neither had those who had worked alongside him, and *nor had he*. So he wanted to get from James the full picture of what came next to put in front of Laura when he returned to the house where he'd felt like a visitor.

It had been at his suggestion that he'd slept in the spare room, not hers. Had she wanted him back in her bed?

But, no, how could she? Only hours before she'd asked him for a divorce. He'd been totally stunned at her request and was praying that it had been a spur-of-the-moment thing that she would change her mind about.

Breakfast was a stilted affair with only the children's chatter to liven it up and when the three of them were ready for the short walk to the village school Laura told him, 'I'll be ready to go to the practice soon. What time do you intend leaving?'

'As soon as I've seen the children safely inside I'll be back for the car. I need to be in London before three o'clock.'

'I'll hang on, then, so that I can lock up once you've gone,' she told him

'Whatever,' he agreed absently as his glance took in the vision she presented in a smart navy suit and white blouse with matching navy footwear, and the fair swathe of her hair swept back into a neat coil. She was so fantastic, he thought achingly. How could he have been so careless with the love they'd had for each other?

The children were tugging at him, with Sophie anxious to show off her father to her friends, and dressed in their neat school uniforms of gold and green and each carrying a small satchel they placed themselves one on either side of him and the trio disappeared in the direction of the village school.

When Gabriel came striding back half an hour later she was standing at the gate, waiting for him, and it felt like a dream. She'd imagined this moment so often, him walking towards her in sunshine, back where he belonged, and now that the time had come it was like groping through fog.

'Have you got everything?' she asked weakly as the shock waves of his nearness washed over her.

He nodded, and after locking up she waited to see what he would do next. Would he just drive off with a brief goodbye after her announcement of the previous night, she wondered, or give her a formal peck on the cheek?

As he bent towards her it seemed as if that was what it was going to be, but not so. His arms reached out to encircle her, his mouth was on hers and he kissed her long and lingeringly before letting her go, then without a word having passed between them he got into the car and drove off in the direction of the motorway that ran past the village.

She put her hand to her mouth. It was the first time he had touched her in any shape or form since that awful day, and she thought despairingly that she'd had to mention divorce for him to show any signs of still wanting her.

Yet he had gone for reasons best known to himself without any mention of when he would see her again. How was she supposed to feel? For now she chose to put her hurt and anger to one side and she set off for another day at the Swallowbrook Medical Practice.

On arriving, she went straight to her office on the lower ground floor and so didn't see Nathan arrive dumbstruck after taking Toby to school.

'I've just seen some guy seeing Laura's children into school,' he told Libby. 'It would seem that the missing father has turned up!'

'Really!' she exclaimed. 'What was he like?'

'That's just it!' he told her with amazement unabated. 'What are they called?'

'Er, Sophie and Joshua?'

'No! I mean their surname. It's Armitage, isn't it?'

'Yes. Why?'

'It was Gabriel Armitage, the cancer specialist, with Sophie and Josh. I've seen his face often enough in medical journals to recognise him. I had no idea that they were connected.'

With her amazement on a level with his she said, 'I recall he hit the headlines a few months back but can't remember what it was about, but it's good to know that Laura has a husband in her life to help her with the children, *and cherish her like you do me*,' she said softly, with the memory of long years of loving the man by her side without any signs from him, until one wonderful day he had returned to Swallowbrook and swept her off her feet.

'I don't think we should say anything to Laura,' she advised. 'Let her tell us about the man in her life in her own time.'

'Sure,' Nathan agreed, with his mind already switched on to the busy day ahead.

As Gabriel approached the hospital that he hadn't seen for many long months, James Lockyer, head of the board of governors, was pacing the boardroom. He was one of the oncologist's closest friends and had been devastated when Gabriel had been sent to prison for the last thing he would have expected him to be guilty of, but he had known the number of hours his friend had put in on the cancer unit with dedicated zeal and it would seem that he'd finally cracked.

When he'd phoned to ask to see him that afternoon James had thought that the hour of reckoning was going to come for Gabriel a second time, but from a different source—the hospital—which meant that his career could be in jeopardy, even though what had happened on that never-to-be-forgotten day had only been connected with his work from a stress point of view.

During all the time Gabriel had been head of oncology there had never been even a second when his expertise and judgement had been questioned, and now because of a split second of anger James was going to have to set the wheels turning that would bring his friend before the hospital board, who would decide whether he should be allowed to continue practising there.

The incident with his next-door neighbour would most likely have passed without notice if the other guy hadn't cracked his head on the fireplace with disastrous results as he'd fallen backwards, and from that had come the court's decision to award a prison sentence.

As the two men shook hands James was aware of the change in his friend. Gabriel had always been a man with a strong sense of purpose. Being shut away hadn't altered that, but there was a grimness about him that had never been there before and as they discussed his future the reason for it became apparent.

'You know that we want you back here as soon as possible, don't you Gabriel?' James said, 'But the wheels of hospital protocol turn slowly and I will have to instigate the usual procedures with regard to the hierarchy coming up with a decision as to whether you should be allowed to continue working here.

'I know how much your work means to you and will move heaven and earth to get you back with us, but I will be only one voice amongst others when the meeting takes place.'

'I understand all of that,' Gabriel told him, 'and will face the music when summoned, but, James, whatever the result it won't make all that much difference to my future plans. I'm giving up medicine and moving to the countryside to be with Laura and the children.

'While I've been away she has moved to a charming lakeside village and I intend to move there to be with my family. It was my neglect of her, due to the job, that started it all, and there is not going to be any more of *that*. Let me know when the "firing squad" wants me up before them and I will be there, otherwise I shall be involved in rural life.'

'I can't believe what you're saying!' James exclaimed. 'You are the best we've ever had and we won't be able to exist without your work.'

'I don't know about that,' he told him, 'but one thing I do know. I can't exist without Laura…and she's just told me that she wants a divorce.'

'Ah, now I understand.' James nodded sombrely. 'But do let the wheels turn with regard to you being allowed to return to medicine one day. You might change your mind at some time in the future when you've put things right with her.'

'I doubt that will happen. It could be the same thing all over again if I do.' Gabriel rose from his chair. 'I'll leave you my phone number so that you can get in touch when I'm needed to face the board. And, James, it's been great to see you.

'I'm going to have a quick word with my team before I go. Jenny, my secretary, and no doubt the rest of them think I'm going to be able to take up where I left off here just like that, so I owe it to them to explain and say goodbye.'

'Yes,' James agreed, 'but it will be a sad day for this place.'

'No one is indispensable. There will be others to come with the same skills as mine. For all I know, they might have already appeared,' he told him, and went to carry out the next painful thing that he had to do, say hello and goodbye to those he'd worked with.

When he arrived back at the town house in the smart London square Gabriel sat star-

ing into space. If someone had told him a
year ago that he would calmly give up practising medicine with no other kind of job
prospects in view, he would have laughed
in their face.

But the fact of it was that he'd had to
make a choice, his career or his family, in
particular his wife, and he knew that he
could just about exist without the one, but
not without the other.

He was going to phone Laura, as he'd
promised, but later when the children were
in bed and when she knew what he'd said to
James, maybe she would change her mind
about wanting a divorce.

The children were asleep and the house was
still around her as Laura thought about the
day that had started with Gabriel actually
being around to take the children to school,
then going back to London as swiftly as he
had come.

He was always happiest there for the very
good reason that it was where the hospital
was, the huge, red-brick magnet that could
always attract him away from her and the

children and would soon be casting its spell over him again if he was allowed to continue practising there after what had happened.

Where was Gabriel now, she wondered, celebrating his freedom somewhere with James, or in a bar with the members of his team? She wouldn't blame him for doing either of those things. He'd been shut away from reality and needed to get back to it.

Though wasn't his idea of reality to see a patient cured, or at the least provide more time for them to enjoy what quality of life he was able to give them?

When the phone rang she was there in an instant, heart beating faster, nerves stretching, but it was Nathan's voice coming over the line to say that the doctors would like to get together with her to discuss some refurbishment of the surgery premises and would she arrange a meeting to that effect?

It rang again shortly afterwards, once again breaking into the silence of the house, and this time it was the voice she wanted to hear.

'I've been to see James to find out what

happens now with regard to my position at the hospital.' Gabriel said, bypassing small talk in order to get to the news he hoped Laura wanted to hear. 'He says there will be a meeting shortly to discuss it, and that in view of my stay in HMP he won't be able to guarantee them agreeing to me taking up where I left off.

'All of which is no surprise, and until I hear more about it from him I will be returning to Swallowbrook some time tomorrow if that is all right with you.'

'Yes, of course,' she told him unsteadily, after trying to take in what he'd been saying. They'd both known that the sentence Gabriel had served could affect his career, but he was in much demand medically, and James would not want to lose him as one of the hospital's top consultants.

When he'd rung off she spent the rest of the evening in a state of acute anxiety. His career was Gabriel's life, she thought desperately.

If he couldn't treat the sick he would be devastated, yet he'd sounded calm enough at the prospect. *But she wasn't*. His job might cost them their marriage if he was allowed to go back to it, yet she couldn't bear the thought of him being separated from it. And what did he mean by announcing his intention to join her and the children here? It was as if their earlier conversation had never happened; he still hadn't responded to her request for a divorce.

The night that followed was not one of peaceful sleep. She tossed and turned and eventually went into the kitchen to make a drink at four o'clock as a midsummer dawn was beginning to lighten the sky, and as she gazed unseeingly to where the lake shimmered on the skyline the thought came that if Gabriel was given the chance to go back to his life's work, a divorce might be the only answer. It would leave him free to follow his calling without his responsibilities to her and the children weighing him down.

She'd told him it was what she wanted in the middle of a hurtful moment, not really meaning it, but maybe in the long run it would be the best thing for all of them if she could endure the agony of a permanent separation. The one that she'd just lived

through, if living was the right word to describe it, had been hard enough to cope
with, and that had been only for a matter
of months.

CHAPTER THREE

WHEN Laura arrived home the following afternoon after collecting the children from school, there was no sign of Gabriel's car on the drive, but he arrived shortly afterwards and relief washed over her. He was back where she could see him, touch him, not shut away like a common criminal.

She'd spent most of the day trying to imagine his conversation with James and her spirits had been at a low ebb, but now that he was back again the dark thoughts were receding, His friend wouldn't let the world of medicine be deprived of Gabriel's contribution to it, she decided.

'I'm so glad you're back,' she told him. Sophie and Josh came running out. 'And so are the children.'

'I told them I would be,' he said with a

tight smile. 'If the traffic hadn't been so bad I would have been in time to pick them up from school. The last thing I want is to upset them by doing another disappearing act.'

They were on the drive where she'd gone out to greet him when she'd seen the car pull up outside and he said, 'Maybe we should go inside to talk rather than discussing our affairs out here. I'll get my stuff in later.'

Once they had closed the door behind them she said sombrely, 'It is awful that you have to justify yourself to these people who can decide your future with just a few words.'

'They won't be doing that, Laura, it's sorted,' Gabriel said, wishing he didn't have to tell her in one way, yet in another he needed to see her reaction when he told her that he was giving up oncology and anything else medical.

He wanted her to know how much he regretted his past fixation with his career and wanted to put things right between them, but before he could explain she was saying joyfully, 'You mean it's all right? You don't have to face any meeting of the board? Your job is safe?'

'Not exactly,' he said slowly, with a sinking feeling inside. 'At this moment I have joined the ranks of the unemployed. I've just told James that I'm quitting.'

'What?' she asked in a strangled whisper. 'It was your life, Gabriel! You can't just walk away from it.'

'Yes, I can,' he told her. 'Before I became a workaholic you and the children were my life, we had a good marriage, were a happy family, but always there was in my mind the longing to try to save others from the same fate as my parents and I let it govern me.

'But not any more. I intend to make up for my neglect of you by being here when you need me, and also when you don't. This place you have moved us to is paradise and I intend to make every moment count.'

'What about your staff?' she asked urgently. 'Your team worship you. What will they say?'

'They know. After I'd told James I went to see them.'

'And how did they react?' she croaked.

'They weren't happy, but I explained that I wouldn't have been able to take up where I'd left off with them for some weeks or even months if I'd intended staying, as it would have depended on the powers that be whether I would still be able to practise, so there you are.'

Yes, there I am, she thought. *Obviously the days are gone when we made life-changing decisions together.*

The nightmare she'd created that day at the hospital was still there, assuming larger proportions all the time, and now there was this awful news that Gabriel was ready to cast his life's work aside because of it.

All it had needed had been a little adjustment in their lives, a little more time spent with her and the children, but it had turned into a monster that was eating up their happiness, *what was left of it.*

'And what are we going to do about the town house?' she asked, as if she cared after what she'd just been told.

'Nothing for the moment,' was the reply. 'It is too early to start making any decisions about that.'

'Yes, whatever,' she agreed wearily, and moving towards the kitchen turned her attention to something less shattering, the preparation of the evening meal.

Dismayed at her reaction to his news, he followed her and framed in the doorway said softly, 'Laura, please don't be like this. Life can only get better without the weight of my job in our lives.' But she carried on peeling and slicing vegetables with her head turned away from him as her hopes for their lives getting back to normal were disappearing with the news of the extreme measures he'd gone to for her sake.

She'd never wanted anything from him except a little more of his time, but Gabriel had given her all of it in one magnificent gesture, and instead of being overjoyed she was horrified.

The atmosphere during the evening was not lively. The meal had been mediocre due to the state of mind of the cook, and Sophie was developing some sort of a virus infection, was hot and fretful, and was for once happy to go to bed.

With nothing they wanted to say to each

other after the painful moments in the kitchen earlier, they went up to bed themselves not long after the children, and once again Gabriel headed for the spare room after he'd checked that Sophie was no worse and was sleeping peacefully. Tonight Laura was relieved that she wasn't going to be sharing a bed with her husband.

The next morning when she went downstairs after a night that had been a mixture of dozing and sleeplessness and checking on Sophie, Laura heard voices and found Gabriel giving the children their breakfast amidst lots of laughter, with his daughter looking better after a good night's sleep.

'What can I get you?' he asked, taking note that she was pale and puffy-eyed. He felt like kicking himself for unloading the news that he was jobless of his own choice the moment they had been together again.

'Just a cup of tea,' she said, and perched down beside the children, who had almost finished eating. She could feel Gabriel's dark gaze on her and turned away. She was in no mood for any further discussion at such an hour and when she'd finished the drink went upstairs to get ready for whatever was waiting for her at the practice.

How he was going to spend his day she didn't know and wasn't going to ask. If he intended staying here with them at Swallows Barn, as he had said he would, their roles were going to be reversed, and it wasn't an unhappy thought to know that she was going to be the one who came and went jobwise, while he took over the role that had been hers in the form of seeing the children to school, shopping, cooking and keeping the house in order.

It hadn't been like that when they had first been married, they'd shared the chores because they'd both had jobs. But when the children had come along and Gabriel's workload had assumed huge proportions, she had fallen into the role of the domestic 'goddess', and although accepting that it was a necessary procedure she had sometimes been reminded of how her mother had been kept tied to household chores by her domineering father, and how she, Laura, had vowed that she was never going to be the same.

But with a husband who was never there the mantle of it had fallen onto her shoulders and now maybe there was going to be a change of plan regarding who did what, and if she read Gabriel's mind right, he wouldn't bat an eyelid.

She was still in a state of shock from his news of the night before, but was adjusting to it, and foremost was the thought that if anyone was due for a fallow period in their lives, he was.

'I'm taking Sophie and Josh to school again and will pick them up this afternoon,' he informed her. 'I have so much lost time to make up with them.'

'Yes, I do know that,' she replied. 'Why not take them for a sail after school? They love being on the lake.'

'What about you?'

She shook her head. 'I have a practice meeting about the refurbishment of the premises this afternoon and can't get away. I won't be home until half past five at the earliest.'

'And what would you have done with the

children if I hadn't been here?' he wanted to know.

'There is an arrangement at the school for those children whose parents can't be there to collect them at the normal home time. Games and refreshments are available to keep them occupied until they arrive.'

'I see.'

He was groaning inwardly, feeling even more surplus than he did already. But Laura had been in a position where she'd had to cope without him while he had been serving his sentence. She'd had to be on the top of things with regard to Sophie and Josh, moving house and going back to administration after being out of it ever since the children had been born.

No doubt her capabilities came from already having been thrust into the role of single parent while he'd been working almost round the clock. Maybe that was the reason why she'd mentioned divorce, the knowledge that she'd already done all the things that it would ask of her.

Sophie and Josh came downstairs at that

moment ready to go and their stilted conversation drifted into silence.

They could have all gone for a sail in the evening if Laura couldn't be with them in the afternoon, he thought as the three of them walked to the school. But he'd been able to tell that she was relieved to be otherwise occupied and would no doubt have had a reason why she couldn't go with them later in the day if he'd suggested it.

The barriers were up. He'd done the wrong thing as far as she was concerned in deciding to give up medicine, even if he *was* given the possible opportunity to take up where he'd left off. He was trying to atone for his neglect but she hadn't seen it that way. She'd obviously thought him reckless and uncaring to unburden himself of his career in such a manner. Never in her darkest moments would she have asked him to do that.

He'd taken the children for a sail on the lake, as Laura had suggested, and as on the other occasions when he'd been with them on his own since arriving in Swallowbrook had enjoyed every moment of the time spent with them.

Was getting to know Sophie and Josh better going to be the silver lining of the dark cloud that had hung over him during past months? he wondered. He'd always been a loving father but because of the job it had been on a limited scale and now there was all the time in the world.

It was half past five and the three of them were walking towards the surgery, eating ice cream cornets. It seemed as if the meeting might be over as the only staff to be seen were Laura and a tall guy chatting on the forecourt.

She was laughing at something he'd said and he realised it was a long time since *he* had made her laugh. Cry, yes, he could do that all right.

When she saw them approaching he watched the colour rise in her cheeks, yet she was in control of the situation and on the point of introducing him to the stranger but she was forestalled by Sophie and Josh crying 'Dr Hugo!' and running up to him as if they knew him well.

'Hello, you two,' he said ruffling Josh's fair mop, while casting a curious glance at the man standing silently just a few feet away.

'Hugo may I introduce my husband, Gabriel Armitage?' Laura said at that moment, and her companion observed him in astonishment.

'Not *the* Gabriel Armitage, the oncologist!' Hugo said, and when he received a nod of acknowledgement went on, 'I am delighted to meet you.'

'My daddy is famous,' Sophie chipped in at that moment, and as the two men shook hands Gabriel thought that 'infamous' would be a better description, but maybe this nice guy hadn't heard about his criminal activities.

'I must go,' Hugo said at that point, as if he felt he had to explain his presence to the silent stranger. 'My wife has gone on ahead to get our evening meal under way. Laura and I were just comparing notes about the meeting that has just taken place.'

Turning to her, he said, 'Do bring Gabriel round for dinner one evening, Laura.

We'd love to have you both if you can find a childminder, or otherwise bring the children with you.' And off he went to Lakes Rise, his house not far away, where his new wife, who he adored, would be waiting for him.

'He seems a decent sort,' Gabriel said as the four of them made their way home.

'Yes, he is,' Laura agreed. 'Hugo made me welcome from the word go when I came here, and helped me to get settled in Swallows Barn. He was married just a short time ago to Ruby, our junior doctor who came from Tyneside to join the practice. She'd lived in Swallowbrook when she was young and had always wanted to be part of the medical team here. With regard to the two of them I think it was love at first sight.'

So Hugo Lawrence *was* a decent sort, as he'd imagined him to be, Gabriel thought, but *he* was the one who should have been there to look after Laura's needs at such a time. Would he ever be free of the feeling of having let her down *over and over again*?

When the four of them had eaten, the children went into the garden to play until it was their bedtime, and noting that her listlessness at breakfast time was still there he said, 'I'll clear away, Laura, while you relax, and maybe when Sophie and Josh are asleep you might feel like continuing our discussion about the future from last night.'

'I won't have time,' she said immediately. 'I need to write up the minutes from today's meeting before I begin getting in touch with contractors and others that we are going to employ to carry out the refurbishment of the practice.'

'Fair enough,' he said evenly. 'In that case, I might go down to the pub when the children are asleep. I can't remember when last I sat behind a glass of beer.'

'Yes, whatever,' she agreed.

He paused in the kitchen doorway on his way to join Sophie and Josh at their play and when she looked up he was frowning. 'I hope that bringing work home from the practice isn't a regular thing. It is a bit much for them to expect that of you.'

'It is my own choice,' she told him. 'Something I do before starting on any chores that need to be done once the children are in bed.'

'I see. In other words, you've got it all

sorted and don't need me around. Is that why you want a divorce?'

She didn't reply. Had something happened to Gabriel's keen perception while he had been shut away from them? She needed him with every beat of her heart, with every breath she took.

What had happened to them had taken the last of the glow from a marriage that had already been fading and she ached for it to be as it used to be, but not at the cost of him giving up medicine, never that!

Gabriel had done what he'd said he might do and had gone to The Mallard where the conversation would be light amongst the visitors and residents who packed the place on summer evenings. There would be noise, laughter and good temper, all a far cry from the home he had just left and the wife who had nothing to say to him.

The children were asleep and it was so quiet Laura felt she would be able to hear a pin drop. The notes she'd made that afternoon were in front of her and with little enthusi-

asm she began to arrange them into a sem-
blance of order, but not for long. The phone
rang and it was James at the other end of
the line.

'Laura!' he said at the sound of her voice.
'How are you?'

'Surviving, James… Just about,' she told
him wearily. 'If you want Gabriel, he has
gone to the pub to find some light relief
from my company.'

'I did want to talk to him,' was the reply,
'but it can wait. You and I haven't spoken
since he was released, have we, and I've
been anxious to know how things are between you. Has Gabriel told you that he's
giving up medicine? Leaving the hospital
whether they want him to stay or not?'

'Yes, he told me last night and I was
devastated for two reasons amongst many,
James. First of all because fighting cancer is his life, he will shrivel and die without it, and secondly because he has made a
decision of such importance without consulting me!'

'That may be so, Laura,' he told her soberly, 'but it was you that he was thinking

of when he did that, not himself. I'm just as upset as you are.

'I feel for both of you, but I also have the cancer unit to concern myself about. The patients and staff here need him, or someone like him.'

'What were his chances of being able to carry on if he had wanted to?' she asked.

'I'm hopeful. I will be pointing out that it wasn't the force of the blow that was struck that nearly killed the other guy. It was the misfortune that the marble fireplace was behind him as he fell backwards, and I will also be reminding the board that Gabriel immediately cast off the mantle of the betrayed husband and stepped back into the role of the lifesaver that he has always been.'

She had to ask. 'Does he still think he was the "betrayed husband"?'

'He has never mentioned it since. I would very much doubt it, but he hasn't said anything to me either, I'm afraid, except that he is filled with remorse about everything that has happened.'

'I have never, ever looked at another man since the moment I met him,' she told him.

'That I can well believe.' And she could tell that James was smiling at the other end of the line. 'He has it all—the looks, the charisma, the beautiful wife and the high-flying career.'

'That is in the past,' she reminded him. *'He hasn't got a career now!'*

She heard the front door click open and with a rapid change of subject said, 'Gabriel is here now, James.' Passing her husband the phone, she picked up the paperwork that she'd been sorting and went to spend another miserable night alone under the covers.

When Laura went down to breakfast the following morning it was the same as the day before, with Gabriel in charge again. Though he had only been back with her and the children a couple of days, already the four of them were slipping into a routine, with him as the house husband and her with the position of practice manager to go to each day. It was ironic that she was now the one involved in health care instead of him.

But she daren't dwell too long on that.

Just the thought of him idling the days away
when he could be treating the sick made her
want to weep, but of course there was the
small matter of whether he would be given
the chance to do that even if he wanted to.

Yet James had been reassuring and she
couldn't resist asking Gabriel if he'd said
the same to him as he'd said to her...that
he was hopeful for a clean slate for Gabriel
as far as the hospital was concerned, because the blow that he'd given their neighbour wouldn't have been enough to cause
serious injury on its own, and that the fireplace had been a contributory factor.

He was engaged in pouring milk onto the
children's cereal and didn't look up until
he'd finished what he was doing. When he
did and their glances locked he said, 'Yes,
he told me all of that, and a few more things
as well, such as I was crazy wanting to leave
medicine. But as I pointed out, *he* hasn't got
a wife who wants a divorce.'

Now was the moment to tell him she
wished she hadn't said that, even though
she'd meant it during the few seconds that
the words had fallen from her lips, but al-

most immediately had regretted them. How could she face a life without Gabriel?

He was turning away to take bread out of the toaster and they were alone, Sophie and Josh had gone into the sitting room to watch TV so the opportunity was there to tell Gabriel that the last thing she wanted was a divorce.

But he'd just been commenting on his proposed departure from the London oncology scene and might think that her change of mind was connected with coaxing him back into cancer care, when all she had ever wanted had been a lighter workload where she and the children saw more of him, where their life was how it used to be, with him holding her close in the night and sharing the occasional meal with them.

With Sophie and Joshua a continual joy, they had planned to have another child, but that idea had been put to one side because Gabriel had always been too tired, and as she had been beginning to feel more and more like a single mother, the thought had lost its appeal.

* * *

Hugo's wife, Ruby, sought Laura out in the middle of the morning at the surgery and said laughingly, 'You are a dark horse, a husband who is a London consultant, and Gabriel Armitage of all people.'

Laura smiled back at her. She liked the slender young doctor with the short, chestnut-coloured hair and ivory skin. It was plain to see that she was much cherished by her new husband, but sometimes she picked up on melancholy in Ruby, though it always disappeared when Hugo came into view.

The two of them, husband and wife, did the weekly antenatal clinic at the surgery and once when someone had asked Ruby jokingly how she would feel when she was pregnant and was doctor and patient at the same time, Laura had seen her turn away as if she hadn't heard the question.

'I just stopped by to remind you that it's Swallowbrook's Summer Fayre on Saturday,' Ruby said. 'Weather permitting, it will be on the village green, otherwise in the church hall. Everyone turns out for it, and as you and your family are newly resident here I thought I would make sure that you knew about it.'

'Thanks for that,' Laura told her. 'We will certainly be there. Sophie and Josh will love it.' *Whether Gabriel would want to go she didn't know, but that was up to him.*

Saturday dawned bright and clear with a summer sun high in the sky, and Laura's spirits lifted. When she'd told Gabriel about the coming event after her chat with Ruby he had shown more interest than she'd expected, commenting that there was something to be said for country life, especially when a beautiful lake was part of the package.

Having always been a city dweller and recently having spent some time in exceptionally depressing surroundings, he was realising just how much he had needed a change of scene from the pressures of what had been his life before this. But always there was the knowledge that he was paying a high price for it and so was Laura. Even relinquishing the career that had been so fulfilling and worthwhile hadn't brought her back into his arms.

He wanted to talk it through with her, clear away the cobwebs and start afresh, but it would seem that the void between them had grown too wide for that. He wanted to talk but she didn't, and the spectre of divorce hung over him like a black cloud.

Yet no one seeing the four of them amongst village folk and visitors on the village green would have guessed that all was not well between the two parents.

Laura's light mood persisted as they wandered amongst carousels and ducking stools, watched Morris dancers, and browsed around stalls selling food and goods made by local people.

Libby and Nathan were there with Toby and when introductions had been made the two young boys stayed together as their parents strolled along, but Sophie didn't leave Gabriel's side, clinging onto his hand tightly. Laura thought that never again must their children be separated from their father, no matter how flat and lifeless their marriage had become.

Meals were being served in the village hall by members of Swallowbrook's Community Association with the vicar's wife in charge, while her husband wandered amongst his parishioners from table to table, chatting and smiling benignly upon them.

When he stopped to have a word beside where they were sitting Laura saw that Gabriel was listening to him intently, and when the vicar had moved on he said, 'Is his voice always so hoarse, Laura?'

'Having only just got to know him I haven't spoken to him very often,' she replied, 'but when I have, yes, it has been like that.'

He was rising from his seat. 'Maybe I should have a word with him,' he murmured, and followed the other man, who, having welcomed all those present, had found himself a quiet spot to have some refreshment of his own.

'My name is Gabriel Armitage,' Gabriel said when he drew level. 'I am an oncologist and would suggest that you make an appointment to see someone about your voice box, just to be on the safe side.' As the vicar observed him in surprise, he added, 'I hope that I'm mistaken, but there could be a problem with the larynx that is making your voice so hoarse. How long has it been like that?'

'Er, quite a while,' came the reply, 'but I have put it down to my doing so much talking. It goes with the job, I'm afraid. Please accept my thanks for your concern. I will most certainly do what you have suggested. There will be a clinic opening soon here in the village that will be treating that sort of thing. Maybe I could see someone there when it is functioning.'

Gabriel shook his head. 'Don't wait. See someone now.' And leaving the vicar looking stunned, he went back to join Laura and the children.

'What did you tell him?' she asked.

'Just that it would be wise to have the hoarseness checked and to do it now. The vicar suggested waiting until the new clinic opens, so he had tuned in to what I was hinting at, although neither of us mentioned the "C" word.

'But I've heard that kind of hoarseness

before. In many cases that is what it has been, and everyone knows that early diagnosis can save lives.'

As they looked across to where the vicar's wife was listening open-mouthed to what her husband had to say, she knew that it wasn't likely that Gabriel would be wrong.

For the rest of the afternoon the four of them strolled amongst the crowds and stopped from time to time while the children went on the various rides and gazed at the sideshows, and Laura thought this was what they'd all been short of, family outings, time together.

But the cost for this to come about had been high for all of them, and they had paid dearly for it. She had asked for just a little of his time and now was getting all of it.

Walking beside her, Gabriel was aware of her every mood swing, every smile, every frown, and asked, 'What is wrong? Do you want to go home?'

'No, I'm fine,' she assured him quickly, and observing Sophie and Josh, who were consuming toffee apples with great relish, she said, 'And I don't think the children are ready to go yet.'

'Not even if we go down to the lake and have our evening meal at one of the restaurants there?'

'Well, maybe if we go for a sail first. Why don't we ask them?'

'Yes,' the two of them chorused when the boat trip was mentioned, so shortly afterwards, with farewells to the surgery crowd, they left the village green and made their way to the lake.

As they boarded the *Swallow*, one of the larger passenger launches, Gabriel observed the fells that encircled the lake, bleak in winter, but on a bright summer day displaying a rugged sort of magnificence that would account for the many who were walking and climbing on their steep slopes and high ledges.

'They are something else, aren't they?' he said. 'A challenge that lots of people won't be able to resist, whether they are experienced enough to go up there or not.'

'Yes,' she agreed. 'Both Nathan and Hugo are involved as doctors with the mountain rescue team when it is called out.' Having mentioned them, she chose the moment to ask, 'Do you think they know about what happened to us? No one has said anything.'

'That doesn't mean that they aren't thinking a lot,' he said dryly. 'But I don't mind people knowing I've been in prison. It's in the past, Laura. When are you and I going to talk about the future?'

The children broke into her thoughts at that moment, pointing to the island where they'd had the picnic, and for the rest of the sail and during the meal at the hotel on the lakeside, the happy family charade continued until they were back at Swallows Barn and the children were in bed.

When she came downstairs after their bathtime Gabriel had taken drinks out into the garden and was waiting for her on the patio. As she lowered herself onto a chair opposite him he said, 'We can't go on like this, with you clamming up every time I want to talk.

'I know that our thought processes are not exactly in harmony at the present time, but never discussing our problems isn't going to make them go away. Surely you understand that.'

'The workings of *your* mind seem to have become very shallow since you've been away from me,' she said soberly. 'You say that we never talk, but what has happened to us making decisions together about the important things in our lives? That is how it has always been until recently.

'So did you come out of medicine to show me how much you love me, or to teach me a lesson? That you had your priorities right when I had to make an appointment to see you, and I hadn't?'

'I can't believe you could think that,' he told her, 'but I suppose I've asked for it, like everything else.' He had risen from his chair and was looking down at her, and as she raised her eyes to his he asked, 'Do you still want a divorce?'

She shook her head. 'No. It might be the best thing for us, Gabriel, but it wouldn't be for the children, Sophie especially. I watched her holding your hand ever so tightly at the Summer Fayre and can't count the number of times she asked for you while you were shut away from us. They need you in their lives all the time, not as a part-time father with visiting rights.'

'But not you? *You* don't need me in *your* life any more?'

'I think we've just about exhausted that topic of conversation,' she told him, standing to face him. 'It has run its course.'

'Maybe,' he agreed, 'but *this* hasn't.' And the next moment he was holding her close, pressing the soft curves of her against the hardness of his chest, and with his hand under her chin he raised her mouth to his and kissed her with a hunger that came from long nights without her in a prison cell and the heavy, reproachful burden of regret that weighed him down.

Laura's legs had gone weak at the sudden onslaught of his passion upon her own yearnings. Any thoughts of resisting were disappearing. It was only when reality with its calm common sense took hold of the moment that she found the will to push him away and tell him breathlessly, 'We're not going to resolve our problems this way, Gabriel.'

As his arms fell away she turned and went back into the house and when he followed without speaking she wished him a frail goodnight and disappeared once more into the room that was beginning to feel like a cloistered cell, knowing that the only man she would ever love would be sleeping just across the landing, and if her passion was at a low level, it would seem that his wasn't.

CHAPTER FOUR

SUNDAY brought with it showers and sunny spells so Laura was content to spend the day indoors with her family. Apart from the weather there were chores to be done and preparations for the coming week to deal with for her and the children.

What Gabriel's plans were for the days ahead in the limbo he had created job-wise, Laura didn't know. He hadn't mentioned looking for any other kind of employment and remembering his comments about the attractions of Swallowbrook, maybe he intended to spend what to him would be a summer idyll in the place. And if he did that, couldn't she be less critical of the decision he'd made about his work with cancer? He'd had little enough opportunity to unwind in the past.

The children loved having him around and his help with the domestic side of things was a relief from having to juggle the position of practice manager with all the other responsibilities that had been hers while he hadn't been with them. It made the job so much more enjoyable and fulfilling.

Whether Gabriel was achieving the same amount of pleasure from his switch from well-known oncologist to stay-at-home husband she didn't know, but he seemed happy enough with the present circumstances in spite of having given up the job she would have thought he would have wanted to do for ever.

If they had been communicating the way they used to in the early days of their marriage she would have been aware of what it was costing him to be shut off from his life's work, but that sort of closeness was missing, and sleeping in separate beds in separate rooms wasn't going to bring it back.

There had been no news from James over recent days and her experience of hospital administration at that level had taught her that committees and that sort of gathering often did what they had to do at snail's pace.

But didn't Gabriel realise that by giving up his consultancy she was being made to feel that she was to blame for all that had happened to them? She would be seen as shallow and selfish, the wife who had felt she should come before his work, when that had not been the case.

When she looked out into the garden he was seated on the patio, reading the Sunday papers in the very same spot where he'd wanted to make love to her the night before, and she felt the sting of tears. That part of their lives had been wonderful once, but not any more, because it had gradually disappeared.

Now there was all the time in the world to make up for it, but on what basis when the foundation of their marriage was crumbling? No way could she face the thought of what had been a magical coming together of tenderness and desire being replaced by lust.

As if he sensed her watching him, Gabriel looked up and the children, who were playing near him, waved. She waved back, and through the open window called to him, 'I'm going to go for a stroll.'

'Do you want us to come with you?' he asked.

'No,' she told him with a smile to take away the sting of the refusal. 'I need some time on my own for a change. Ever since the children and I moved to Swallowbrook it is something that has been in short supply, what with caring for them, starting a new job, the renovating of this place, and so forth.'

'Yes, I can imagine,' he said bleakly, with the agonising memory of long nights when he'd imagined her alone with the children and no one to protect her, should the need arise. Yet he hadn't exactly been around that much before then, had he?

Sometimes the night had been almost over before he'd wearily climbed the stairs with sleep the only thing on his mind. So Laura must feel that a vacant place in the bed here in Swallowbrook wasn't all that different from how it had been before.

She was waiting for anything else he had

to say before she went for the stroll she'd mentioned and he didn't disappoint her. 'Being alone is the last thing I would crave,' he told her. 'I've spent enough time under those conditions to last a lifetime.'

'Yes. I know,' she told him wretchedly.

What he had endured because of her would be engraved upon her heart for ever, and instead of leaving Gabriel and the children for a while with a light step, her feet felt heavy and leaden as she left the house.

When the lake came into view she walked alongside it until she was away from the bustle of the boat terminal, and perching on a dry stone wall that separated the lakeside from one of the many farms in the area she let the quiet of the place wash over her. Maybe here with no one to make any demands of her, or to confuse her further, she would be able to get a clearer perspective of the future, she decided, but it didn't happen. She just sat gazing blankly into space, letting time drift by.

Back at the house Gabriel was doing the opposite, watching the clock. Laura was taking some stroll, he was thinking. The amount of time she'd been gone indicated a much longer exercise than that. He'd given the children their evening meal and they would soon be ready for bed, but not before their mother came back. If she didn't come soon, he would go and look for her and it would mean him having to take them with him.

When the doorbell rang he wasn't expecting it to be her, she would have a key, and neither was he prepared to see Ruby and Hugo Lawrence standing in the porch.

'Hello, Gabriel,' Hugo said. 'We just stopped by to ask if Laura is here with you. We've just been for a sail on one of the passenger launches and we thought we saw her sitting by the lakeside as we passed. It is so rarely that she is alone when out and about, so we thought that if we found her at home with you we were mistaken.'

'Come in,' he said, and they stepped into the hallway. 'No, she isn't here. Laura went for a stroll ages ago, saying she wanted some breathing space, some time to herself, and hasn't returned, so I was just about to go in search of her. If you could describe exactly where you saw her I'll go and bring her back. It could be that she's walked too far, or maybe hurt her foot or something, and she hasn't got her phone with her. She left it on the kitchen table.'

The children had heard Hugo's voice and were coming running at the sound of it, and Ruby said, 'You go, Dr Armitage. We'll stay with Sophie and Josh until you get back.'

'Thanks, I appreciate the offer,' he told her, and was behind the driving seat of the car in seconds, praying that he would find Laura where they'd said, or even nearer home if possible.

She'd been pushed too far, he thought grimly as the lake came into view, and he was to blame. He'd thought that by giving her *all* of his time she would understand how much he regretted what had happened to them, but again he'd miscalculated her love for him, and the sacrifice he'd made felt hollow when memories of the satisfaction that came from his kind of work came back to haunt him.

When he turned the car on to the last few

yards of road that led to the lake she was there, walking slowly towards the home that she'd made for them, and his heart leapt with thankfulness.

She looked pale and heavy-eyed but she was safe and as she got into the car the first thing she asked was, 'Where are the children? You haven't left them alone, have you, Gabriel?'

He smiled and felt as if his face would crack with the effort as he commented wryly, 'You should know me better than that. Your friends Ruby and Hugo Lawrence are with them. I asked them to sit with the children while I came to find you. You've been gone for ages, I was getting worried.

'Why did you stay out so long? I've been going crazy, wondering where you were. I thought maybe I'd pushed you too far, or at the least you were in no hurry to get back to me.'

'It was so quiet and peaceful where I was,' she explained, 'and instead of doing some uninterrupted thinking, which was what I'd intended, I fell into the best sleep I've had in days.'

When the car pulled up on the drive the door opened and the children were there with Hugo and Ruby smiling their relief to see Laura safely back where she belonged.

They didn't know the exact circumstances of Gabriel Armitage's sudden appearance in Swallowbrook, but remembered from way back that there had once been a court case that he'd been involved in.

But now, having met the man himself, they could not believe that it had been anything too disastrous because his manner and appearance spoke of integrity, and in the medical world his name was revered by all who'd had cause to seek him out for help. That he loved his family was also plain to see. He doted on his children and his anxiety with regard to Laura's non-appearance after her walk was proof of how much he cared for his wife.

Her smile of greeting for her friends was apologetic. 'I am so sorry you've been troubled on my account,' she told Hugo and Ruby. 'I'd gone for a walk and when I stopped to rest by the lake I fell asleep and didn't wake up for ages.'

'We didn't mind keeping an eye on Sophie and Josh,' Ruby said gently. 'Gabriel
was so concerned that you hadn't come
back, but all is well now, isn't it?'

I wish, Laura thought, but her reply was
reassuring enough to put Ruby and Hugo's
concerns to rest. 'Yes. It's fine. So can I
make you a cup of tea or coffee, or get you
a cold drink?'

'No, thanks,' Hugo said. 'Sophie has done
the honours. We've all had an iced lolly out
of the fridge and enjoyed it immensely, so
we'll be off and leave you folks to enjoy
what is left of the weekend. We'll see you
in the morning, Laura.'

'Yes, you will,' she assured him con-
fidently, the job being in a different
compartment of her life, where all was un-
complicated and rewarding.

When they'd gone she made a meal for
Gabriel and herself while he saw to bedtime
for the children.

When he came downstairs afterwards he
said levelly, 'James called whilst you were
out. The board won't be meeting for some
time because it's midsummer and holiday

time. Some of them disappear for weeks on end, so it isn't going to be yet that your concerns will be answered one way or another.'

Laura put down her knife and fork slowly and looking directly at him asked, 'What about *your* concerns, Gabriel? Don't *you* have any?'

Oh, yes! He had them all right but wasn't going to voice them. Every time he thought about giving up medicine, especially in the form that he excelled in, it was like a knife in his heart, but his neglect of his family had an even greater effect.

As he met Laura's cool, questioning glance, his thoughts went back to the time when there had been no clouds in their sky, when the beautiful eyes that now were cold had melted with her love for him.

It had been a time that when night came and the children were asleep that they'd made love, and afterwards she'd slept safe and secure in his arms.

Now she went in and closed her bedroom door on him and he felt that he hadn't the right to protest.

'Yes, I have concerns, Laura, but they're

coming from a different direction from yours and they won't go away until I see the way ahead clearly.'

After that Laura felt there was nothing left to say and they finished the meal in a silence that lasted until the summer dusk closed in on them.

The next morning there was little time for talking, with dinner money for the children to be sorted and school uniforms to be found.

When Sophie and Josh were ready for Gabriel to walk them to school once more, he paused in the doorway and said, 'Will you still be here when I get back?'

'Possibly,' she informed him, 'but it will only be for a matter of minutes. I have a pharmaceutical rep due at ten o'clock. She's from one of the big companies and calls quite frequently, which is something that might be going to change, as the general feeling at the surgery is that the attraction was Hugo Lawrence, and now that he has got his heart's desire in Ruby we may not see so much of her.'

The children were waiting for him at the gate and he said, 'I just want a quick word, that's all.'

'Yes, all right, then,' she agreed, and thought it was more than she did. She hadn't slept a wink for thinking about their exchange of words from the night before.

When he came back, striding along the road where Swallows Barn stood amongst green lawns and a background of trees that were heavy with the bright green leaves of summer, Laura was hovering at the gate, ready to leave for work. But not in so much of a hurry that she didn't have time to dwell for a moment on the attractions of the husband who had become an unpredictable stranger during their months apart.

He was tall and trim, with hair dark and thickly curling, and hazel eyes that used to light up when he saw her, but were now guarded and unreadable.

When he stopped beside her Gabriel said, 'Sorry to keep you waiting. I met the vicar as I was coming away from the school. He was on his way to the surgery to see Nathan Gallagher with regard to what I said to him on Saturday and wanted to chat for a moment. I do hope that I am wrong about the hoarseness.'

'But you don't think you are?'

'No, unfortunately, but you need to be on your way and all I wanted to say was that I regret burdening you with the news from James after the stress of yesterday evening. It could have waited as nothing is going to be happening soon.'

She loved him in that moment, loved his consideration for her feelings when the greater pain at the delay must surely be his.

Reaching out, she took his hand in hers and squeezed it gently, and with all the complexities of their lives put to one side told him, 'Regret is an awful word, Gabriel, and we've both had cause to think it and say it. Can we come to an agreement not to use it any more?' As his eyes widened she gave his hand one more squeeze and set off for the practice with a lighter heart than before.

Gabriel planned to go shopping that morning, something else that he'd had little time for before. Their wedding anniversary was

only a few weeks away and he was hoping
that the occasion might be as special now
as it used to be, that it might be a time for
new beginnings, and with that thought in
mind he drove into the nearby town to buy
an eternity ring.

He chose a circlet of diamonds on a gold
band and he asked the jeweller for an engraving on the inside. He left the shop satisfied with his purchase and hoped that Laura
would feel the same when he presented the
ring to her.

He'd never forgotten their anniversary in
spite of the glow fading from their marriage, but sometimes flowers, or a night at
the theatre, had been arranged by his secretary, and he'd hoped on those occasions that
if Laura had guessed, she hadn't felt that he
loved her any less.

This occasion was going to be different.
He had time to arrange something special,
time for lots of things, but it always seemed
that she hadn't, and aware that the tables
had turned he wondered how she felt about
being the career person while he spent his

time with Sophie and Josh and kept the household running in an orderly fashion.

Laura had seemed to soften when they'd spoken briefly before she'd left for the practice that morning. Was it the beginning of the end of the cold war and now both of the girls in his life were going to be happy?

Whilst he had no worries about Josh, Sophie was very different. Intelligent, quick to pick up an atmosphere, and lost until he had come back into her life.

He would never forget her expression when he'd appeared on the island, the moment of blank uncertainty before she'd called his name and flung herself into his arms as if she'd thought she would never see him again.

They'd kept her young mind free of the truth about his time in prison, but maybe it would have been better if she'd known where he was and had understood that was why he wasn't with them.

But she was fine now, happy and content that he was back with them, and he intended that that was how she was going to stay. He'd given up his career not just for

Laura but for the children's sakes too, and
he could just about exist without it as long
as the three of them were happy.

But with regard to his wife there might be
a long way to go before that happened. She'd
seemed loving towards him earlier on, but
had it been because she was sorry for him?

In her basement office where the comput-
ers and patients' records were kept, Laura's
busy day was under way and she was grateful for it, as for a few hours it would keep
other thoughts at bay.

In a few weeks' time a heavily pregnant
Libby would be leaving the practice after
spending all her working life there, and as
practice manager Laura was in the process
of arranging a farewell party for the con-
tented mother-to-be on the Saturday night
after her last Friday at work.

At the same time discussions were taking
place about finding Libby's replacement.

Also the refurbishment of the surgery
was due to start during the coming week
and unless organised properly would cause
chaos for staff and patients alike. She had

arranged that most of the work would be done in the evenings and at the weekends when the place was closed and that way hoped to bring confusion down to a minimum, but it was still going to be a big undertaking.

The pharmaceutical rep had been and with Hugo so obviously enchanted with his new wife hadn't stayed long, but had managed to get in a comment to the effect that she wouldn't have thought that a pale-faced beanpole would have been his type.

Back at the house Gabriel had received a phone call from Nathan. 'Well spotted with the vicar's hoarseness,' he said. 'We could do with you around permanently, Gabriel. Have you heard about the clinic that will be opening shortly at the side of the surgery?'

'Yes, I have,' he told him, 'but my life is rather complicated at the moment. I've just finished a prison sentence for GBH. It was a man who was taking advantage of Laura and I accidentally injured him quite seriously.'

'I knew there was something,' Nathan

said, 'and I have to say that I would probably have done the same if it had been
someone coming on to Libby. I'll keep my
fingers crossed for you, Gabriel. It would be
a shame for your abilities to be put on hold
for any length of time.'

When they'd finished the call Gabriel
stood gazing into space.

What would Nathan have thought if he'd
told him that he had already *prevented himself* from practising and it was raw agony?

The thought of it was unbearable. It was
his life, the fount of his existence, but so
were his family and his past neglect of them
had been unpardonable, so much so that he
was determined that Laura was going to get
back her confidence in him no matter what.

He spent the early afternoon tidying up
the garden and before he went to collect the
children went up to have a shower in the en
suite in the master bedroom.

A robe that Laura was using hung behind
the door and he held it against his cheek for
a moment. It smelt of the bath essence she
used and his throat closed up. Apart from
the two occasions when he'd kissed her, un-

able to hold back even though he'd sensed resistance in her, there had been no other physical contact between them. Losing his career was bad, but losing Laura was much much worse.

When he arrived at the school he was told that Sophie's teacher wanted a word with him, and leaving Josh chatting to Toby in the playground where he was waiting to be picked up by either Libby or Nathan, he went into the empty classroom where she was waiting and observed her questioningly.

'We had a little upset this afternoon with Sophie,' she explained, 'so I thought I'd better have a word, Dr Armitage. We tried to contact you, but you weren't around at the time.'

'What was it?' he asked. 'My daughter is very happy here and so is Josh.'

'Yes. I know,' she told him, 'and we are pleased about that.'

He was frowning. 'So?

'Sophie fell in the schoolyard during playtime this afternoon and was quite shaken with the impact. She kept asking for you but we couldn't get hold of you, and she became distraught.'

'So didn't you try her mother? Laura works at the surgery.'

'Yes. She came immediately and offered comfort and Sophie gradually calmed down.'

'And was she hurt?' he asked anxiously.

'No. It was just shock, we think. When her mother left she took her back to the surgery with her, and when you've collected Josh you will find Sophie waiting for you there.'

He nodded. 'Thank you for looking after my daughter,' he told her, and went to seek out Josh with the feeling that he'd been congratulating himself too soon with regard to Sophie's need of him. It was still there in her young mind, the fear that he might disappear again. If that wasn't enough to tell him that here in Swallowbrook was where he needed to be, he didn't know what was.

'Why didn't you come when Sophie wanted you?' Josh asked as they made their way to the surgery.

The school must have phoned while he'd

been cutting the grass. The noise of the lawnmower was enough to drown all normal sounds, or maybe it had been while he'd been under the shower.

Whatever the reason, Laura had been brought in to deal with Sophie's upset and must be wondering why he hadn't been around.

When they arrived at the surgery his tension slackened. They found Sophie in Reception, chatting to one of the nurses, who told him smilingly that his daughter had been telling her that she wanted to be a doctor like him.

Not if I can help it, he thought grimly as the three of them went down to where Laura was working in the basement.

'I am so sorry about that,' he told her in a low voice. 'I was cutting the grass. The mower drowns out all noise and I never heard the phone.

'I thought that Sophie's fears had been put to rest but it seems I was mistaken.'

'It was the shock of the fall that triggered it,' she told him evenly, 'and when you didn't appear to offer comfort, her con-

fidence in you being around took a back-
ward step, but she's fine now. I wouldn't
mention it if I were you. I've checked her
over and there doesn't appear to be any sign
of injury so you can relax.'

'Yes, but can *you*?' he said stiffly. 'I know
you're busy at the moment with all sorts of
projects, and having to chase round to the
school won't have helped things along with
regard to that.'

'The fact that I enjoy the challenge of
working here doesn't mean that I've forgotten where my priorities lie,' she said
chidingly, and when the phone rang at that
moment he didn't get the chance to ask what
his rating was amongst them.

Gathering the children to him, he pointed
the three of them in the direction of Swallows Barn and home, and took Laura's advice with regard to Sophie's upset by not
mentioning it as she seemed to have forgotten all about it.

But he hadn't. It didn't alter the fact that
the distress caused by his long absence previously hadn't entirely disappeared, and if
Laura's calm handling of the incident had

overtones of it all being part of a day in her life, was it surprising?

Added to that was Josh wanting to know why he hadn't been there when Sophie needed him, as if he, Gabriel, at that moment, was outside the safe circle that Laura had created for the three of them.

When she arrived home at the end of her working day he expected that the first thing she would do was check on Sophie, who was on her swing in the garden, but to his surprise she came straight to where he was and said in a low voice, 'Have you recovered from Sophie's upset?' She glanced at their daughter. 'It would seem that *she* has. I did feel for you, Gabriel,' adding with a smile that took the sting out of her next comment, 'But that's the price of popularity, I'm afraid.'

He sighed. 'The main thing is that she wasn't hurt. That was all I was concerned about at the time, but it does mean that she still has some feeling of insecurity where I'm concerned and I can't bear that any more than I was able to bear being shut away from the three of you.'

'So why don't we see if Ruby and Hugo will sit in for us for an hour when we've eaten?' she suggested. 'Sophie likes Hugo so she won't be fretting about where you are. The two of us could go for a sail or a stroll by the lake and still be back before their bedtime.'

He was observing her in surprise. 'That would be great if they can manage it, but it's very short notice, Laura. Are you feeling sorry for me because I can't put a foot right with any of my family and are prepared to give me some of your time? Even Josh wanted to know why I hadn't been there when Sophie needed me.'

'Yes, I do want us to have a brief time on our own,' she told him, 'and, no, it isn't because I feel sorry for you. You're far too capable to invite sympathy, but you've had a bad day.'

'I won't argue about that,' he replied. 'So, are you going to ring Ruby?'

'Yes, I'll do it now.' And seconds later she told him, 'They will be round in an hour, which will give the four of us time to have our meal and clear away before they come. Ruby said we needn't rush back as Hugo is the tops when it comes to reading bedtime stories.'

CHAPTER FIVE

THERE were no tears or protests when they left the children with Ruby and Hugo later that evening. The young ones knew them well enough, especially Hugo, to be happy in their care, and as Laura and Gabriel left the house with instructions from their child-minders not to rush back, it had been such a long time since there had just been the two of them that for a few moments they were lost for words, until Laura spoke.

'There is an open-air band concert to-night at the far end of the lake. You like that kind of thing, don't you?'

'Yes,' he replied, 'but not tonight. We've too much catching up to do. It's like being on a first date but with baggage in the form of my stay at Her Majesty's pleasure and a marriage that is floundering.'

'I didn't suggest we spend some time together going over old wounds,' she said flatly. 'I was hoping we could put them all behind us for a while.' She pointed to woods, scented and silent at the bottom of one of the fells that swept down to the lake.

The evening sun was still warm and as they lounged on grass beneath the trees Laura was happy to have him to herself for a little while, and she lay back and smiled up at him. It was a mistake. The dark hazel eyes looking into hers were warming as he said softly, 'Laura, when I said it was like a first date I wasn't expecting this sort of thing to be on the agenda.'

He had rolled over and was looking down on to her and she said, 'If you mean what I think you mean, Gabriel, it wasn't, isn't, because it would be just sex. For us it was never like that. I brought you here where we would be quiet and undisturbed to have a short time of peace in our lives, and if by me lying on the grass I gave out the wrong signals, I'm sorry.'

'Don't be,' he said levelly. 'I've never forced myself on you and am not going to start now. But I rather think we've exploded the peace and quiet that you had in mind, and my determination is that we should discuss our problems, so let's go, shall we?'

Knowing that he was right, she got slowly to her feet and they travelled back the way they'd come in a silence that was only broken when they arrived back at the house, where Ruby and Hugo were waiting to inform them that after lots of fun in the garden their children had been successfully put to bed.

As they thanked them for their efforts neither Hugo nor Ruby was aware that the evening had been yet another hiccup on the way to peace between them.

The next morning the sun was still out to charm them and as soon as the children had eaten they were out in the garden, while their parents dined at a slower pace.

It was Saturday and would seem like an eternity if they didn't find something interesting to do, Laura thought, but after the misunderstandings of the night before there wasn't a lot she could think of that would lighten the atmosphere, and in no time at all Sophie and Josh were tired of the garden and wanting to go somewhere else.

'Libby and Nathan are spending the weekend on the island,' she told Gabriel. 'They have invited us to call if ever we are sailing in that direction and I'm sure the children would like that.'

She wouldn't. It would bring back the memory of his return to their world, unexpected and unannounced while they had been having their picnic, but there was no need for him to know that.

He had been quiet and remote ever since Sophie's upset. She had soon forgotten it, but Gabriel hadn't. It had been a reminder that past insecurities hadn't entirely been forgotten where his daughter was concerned, and Laura's hurts were something he lived with on a daily basis.

Only Josh, happy in his new life with his new friend, seemed to have come out of the painful past without hurt. Laura's suggestion the night before that they ask Ruby and Hugo to child-sit had lifted his spirits, but after it had turned out to be a non-event the remoteness was back.

Aware of it, Laura wasn't sure what his reply would be to the suggestion and was surprised when he said, 'Yes, why not? Why don't we take one of the passenger launches and stop off at the island for a while? Then pick up another of the boats at the landing stage there and sail to the marina for an early dinner.'

'That would be lovely,' she agreed, with spirits lifting, and he smiled a brittle smile.

She rang Libby and Nathan to ask if it was convenient for them to call and was assured that they would be most welcome, so with Josh running on ahead, eager to be with Toby again, and Sophie skipping along between her parents, they set off for the family outing that would occupy most of the day.

While the children played with Toby, and the two women talked babies, Nathan took Gabriel to one side and told him a bit more about the cancer care clinic that was being built.

'Where it stands and the land all around it used to belong to Libby's parents, who had it as a farm. The practice premises were the farmhouse and the land was where the animals were kept.

'When her mother died her father lost interest in the place. He let it gradually fall into a very poor state and had to sell it, and as the previous practice building was becoming too small for the ever-increasing number of patients, my father, who was in charge at that time, bought the farmhouse and the land to provide a new medical centre in the village, so it is seen as the ideal place to build the clinic, right on our doorstep, which couldn't be better as far as we are concerned.'

'I think it's a terrific project, quite cutting edge in its own way,' Gabriel told him.

'I know you have the hearing hanging over your head, but we could really use a man with your expertise. There won't be any decisions made with regard to staffing the new clinic until the late autumn,' Nathan told him, 'though, of course, they will have to start interviewing soon, but I'll keep you informed.'

'I would appreciate that,' said Gabriel. 'They are dragging their feet at the London end, which doesn't maker life any easier as I have Laura and the children to consider and whatever I decide it has to be right for them.'

Libby announced that lunch was ready at that moment so any further discussion had to be put on hold, and when the two families had eaten and the children had gone back to their play it was inevitable that the conversation turned to the practice, with three of the adults present working there.

Nathan informed Gabriel, 'The vicar has had the necessary tests done on his throat and there is cancer of the larynx, so he's being treated with radiotherapy as a first option. There has been no mention of surgery so far, but time will tell, as it always does.

'I imagine that he wants to thank you for your quick diagnosis and said he intends calling on you in the near future. He is fervently hoping that he won't lose his voice.' As Laura listened to what he was saying, the thing that was eating away at her was back. When it came to intensive treatment or surgery Gabriel would be missing from the ranks of oncology if he didn't change his mind about giving it up, *if those who decided such things from a practising point of view didn't do it for him.*

She would not have asked that sort of sacrifice from him, never had, never would. All she had wanted that day at the hospital had been that he should not forget that she was part of his life just as much as his patients, that she loved him and was willing to share him with them, would endure anything, except being ignored.

They stayed on the island with Libby and Nathan for a couple of hours then, feeling that they'd butted into their weekend long enough, picked up the next passing launch and sailed to the marina.

To anyone observing them they were an attractive family with the mother golden haired, blue eyed, and the boy by her side with a similar colouring. While the father, darkly attractive, was holding the hand of a girl child who was unmistakably his.

There was the choice of a fast-food eating place at the moorings or a smart restaurant that Gabriel was observing approvingly, and almost as if they were back to the old days for a moment Laura said laughingly, 'I think that our two young ones would go for chicken nuggets and chips with a can of fizzy drink, in preference to the kind of dishes that were our favourites...if you remember.'

His gaze was holding hers. Of course he remembered. His imprisonment hadn't been that long.

That evening they sat in silence on the patio after the children were asleep, watching the sun set over the lake and the outlines of the surrounding fells darken as the light began to fade. It was the kind of moment that once would have brought Laura into his arms, but the memory of the night before and all the other painful moments that had gone before it was still heavy upon her, and leaving Gabriel sitting in the summer dusk she went hopefully to let sleep blot out the uncertainties of the present.

* * *

The morning of their wedding anniversary dawned with grey skies above and when Laura drew back the curtains and saw the weather she sighed. The day wasn't going to be like times in the past when there had been flowers and presents, going out for a meal, and magical lovemaking, but it would have helped if the sun had been shining and lightened it a little.

Over the last few years the occasion had become less memorable because of Gabriel's workload, but he'd never actually forgotten it, even if he had been pushed to the limit and his secretary had been brought in to see to the arrangements.

Laura hadn't minded that too much, had understood the pressures he had been under. Until the unsatisfactory lives they had been living domestically had caught up with them.

She had something to give him to celebrate the occasion and was hoping he wouldn't read anything into it that wasn't there. Other than it was a large studio photograph of her and the children in a beautiful silver frame.

When she'd had it done she'd thought that he could read into it what he liked, that it was a reminder of their presence in his life, or a memory of a certain stage in the growth of their children to look back on in later years, or even as a flashback to when she'd made the totally preposterous demand for a divorce.

She gave it to him as soon as they met up in the kitchen before Sophie and Josh appeared for breakfast and as he gazed at it for a split second she saw the raw hurt in him, but it was gone in a flash and he said, 'When did you have this taken?'

'It was taken while you were away from us.'

'Ah, yes, I remember,' he said, with his voice softening. 'And I told you not to bring it for me to look at as it would have hurt too much, seeing the three of you so near in the photograph but so far away in reality.'

Without any further comment he began to start the preparations for breakfast. Feeling even less celebratory after that little chat, which hadn't included any signs of what Gabriel had thought fitted the occasion as a gift for her, she went up to wake the children on what was their last day of the summer term.

As Laura walked to the practice some time later the thought was there that the situation between her and Gabriel wasn't being helped by the stress of what was happening workwise.

The refurbishment was under way and not going well, *far from it*.

She was uneasy about the expertise of the small local firm chosen by the doctors to do the work. New to the area, she had gone along with their suggestion and was now wishing she hadn't.

Although the builder in charge and his two assistants were a likeable trio, she felt that there were too many tea breaks, too much chatting amongst them, and knew that irrespective of who had given them the contract it was she as practice manager who in the end was responsible for satisfactory completion of the work.

When she'd exchanged chaste kisses with

Gabriel before she'd given him the photograph, she'd been determined that the evening ahead would have some lightness to it, even though it might lack the magic of earlier years, and as the day progressed had managed to get to the hair salon in the village in the lunch hour and fit in a manicure at the same time.

If Gabriel wanted her in his bed tonight she would be there for him, she vowed, and would forget for a few hours her hurts and yearnings.

She was the last one to leave the surgery at the end of the day. It had been a quiet afternoon for once, the contractors had left and so had the surgery staff. It was only when she was about to lock the door that she became conscious of water beneath her feet.

'Oh, no!' she groaned. 'Not tonight of all nights!' Even as she said it she was reaching for the nearest phone to get the builder back, and received no immediate answer.

When at last his voice came over the line and she explained what was happening, he seemed to have no immediate sense of urgency and merely said, 'Turn the stop tap off, Mrs Armitage, and I'll check the water pipes in the morning.'

'You will look at them *now*!' she told him with deadly calm, 'or you will be sacked!'

That got through to him and shortly after that the three of them turned up and announced that they'd been renewing pipework that afternoon and might have made a wrong connection.

'So put it right, then!' she told them. 'And then maybe I can go home to my family.'

They did as she'd asked but it was not to be a rapid repair and when she rang Gabriel with the hands of the surgery clock on half past seven to tell him that she would be at least another hour, she was hoping that he hadn't set too much store on this special day in their lives and so wouldn't be too disappointed at the delay in her homecoming.

It was hard to tell how he actually did feel when he answered her call. He just said flatly, 'So how long have the repairs been going on and why aren't Nathan and Hugo there to see to it? Have you told them what's happening?'

'I can't get hold of either of them,' she told him. 'It's a lovely evening, they're probably making the most of it somewhere, *and I am the practice manager, Gabriel*. I can't leave the building until I'm sure that there will be no more leakage.'

'Yes, sure,' he agreed. 'So I'll see you about eight-thirty, then.'

'Hopefully, yes,' she replied, and rang off.

The children were asleep. The table was set with the best china and cutlery, candles were glowing in the centre of it, and it was almost nine o'clock.

No mean cook, Gabriel had made chicken parfait for the first course. It was one of their favourite dishes, and for dessert he intended to produce brandy-snap baskets filled with strawberries and topped with clotted cream.

What was missing was Laura sitting opposite him, sharing the meal, with the ring he had chosen for such an occasion on her finger, *but it wasn't happening like that*.

Their lives had turned full circle, he thought wryly. *He* was waiting for *her* to come home from whatever was keeping her job-wise. *She* was the one delayed by necessity, not as serious by far as the things that had prolonged his working day, but the change of circumstances was there, not to be ignored.

How many times must she have gone through this scenario and ended up leaving a note to say that his meal was in the oven, and then gone to sleep beside the empty space where he should have been?

When she came dashing up the drive a few seconds later, mortified to think that their wedding anniversary had ended up as much of a non-event as everything else in their lives at the present time, he met her at the door and as she stood panting in the hallway told her, 'It's all right, Laura. These things happen. The food I've prepared will be past its best, but the wine is still chilled and the flowers haven't yet started to droop.'

'No, I'm the one who's drooping,' she said wearily, 'drooping with fatigue brought on by the carelessness of others.'

He knew immediately that it wasn't the right moment to give her the ring. She'd had a catastrophic evening and was exhausted. Cries of delight would not be on the menu, so the jeweller's box stayed out of sight.

He had flowers and chocolates waiting for her, so she would know he hadn't forgotten, but the chance to show her how he really felt had been knocked sideways, as had the food, and the atmosphere he'd tried to create.

When she went into the dining room and viewed the effort he'd made to celebrate the occasion Laura was gripped by a sick feeling of dismay.

'Are you going to dish out the food?' she asked softly as tears pricked.

'Just help yourself,' was the reply. 'I'll see you at breakfast' As her mortification increased, he left her to it, and seconds later she heard the front door close behind him.

Once outside Gabriel walked towards where the lake slapped peacefully against age-old stone, and stood looking out across it as darkness fell, bringing with it moon and stars, and into the midst of his tangled thoughts came the memory of the place that had been his second home back there in London, the operating theatre.

The smell of it was in his nostrils, he could almost taste the tension that was always present, and every part of him needed to be there again, but tonight's fiasco brought about by Laura being late home had been the climax of all his recent observations about what life must have been like for her before their roles had been reversed.

Turning, he went swiftly back the way he had come, praying that she might still be up so that he could tell her there would be another night, another moment to share, when they might begin to find the way back to where they had once been.

When he arrived back at the house the routine was in place. There was no sign of her and her bedroom door was shut. But one thing was different: there were two notes on the kitchen worktop.

The first one said that she was so sorry that her job at the practice had spoiled the occasion, that she had enjoyed the food immensely, it had been delicious, and it would have been even more enjoyable if he'd been there. *And had he ever thought of becoming a chef?*

It had been a light-hearted comment with an undertone of having accepted that he wasn't going back to medicine, and he smiled a grim smile.

The second missive was to explain that she intended going early to the surgery in the morning to check that all was in order with regard to the building work before the day began, so she wouldn't be joining them for breakfast. Disappointed that the day had ended so badly after a shaky start, Gabriel turned out the lights and headed off upstairs himself to spend his anniversary alone.

Laura had kept to her decision of the night before and was nowhere to be seen when he went downstairs the following morning. But when he drew back the curtains he caught a glimpse of her striding purposefully down the road, looking neat and trim in one of the smart suits she wore for the job, and his thoughts of the night before by the lake came back. Now it was *her* turn to be gone for the day before *he* was awake.

* * *

When she arrived at the surgery all was in order, with the workmen already on the job, and it seemed that there had been no further leaks during the night.

'I called back to check at two o'clock in the morning just to be on the safe side,' the boss said, 'and everything was okay.' As if aware that their lack of speed, carelessness and long lunch breaks might lose them the contract, he followed it with, 'We're going to forge ahead with it today and hope to be finished soon by working over the weekend like you asked us to.'

'Good,' she said absently, with her thoughts on Gabriel, Sophie, and Josh breakfasting without her. She had looked in on the children before leaving the house. Both of them had been sleeping peacefully, and she'd paused for a moment outside the door of Gabriel's room, but that was all it had been, just a fragment of time filled with longing before she'd set off for the day ahead.

A short meeting with the doctors to explain the trauma of the previous night before the day got under way had Nathan all for sacking the workforce on the spot, but Hugo said with his usual calm reasoning that as the refurbishments were almost completed they should allow them to finish but keep a close eye on the amiable trio, and once it was done have all the work checked over by their insurers before settling the account.

After that had been agreed upon, Laura carried on with the duties of the day and tried not to think about how Gabriel must have felt about his wasted efforts of the night before.

She'd sat gazing at the untouched food for ages after he'd gone and then, not wanting to cause him any further hurt, had eaten her fill of it and left a note to say how much she had enjoyed it.

When she arrived home that evening at the correct time he asked, 'So no more leaks or other hiccups?'

She managed a smile. 'No, none. The timing was all wrong, wasn't it?'

'Just a bit,' he agreed, 'but that was yesterday. Today I have had major heart surgery.'

'What?' she gasped.

Unbuttoning his shirt, he displayed a long white strip of material wrapped tightly around him and spattered with tomato ketchup.

As she laughed at the spectacle Sophie appeared with Josh close behind. 'We've been playing at doctors and nurses,' she announced with matron-like precision, and as he gave a theatrical groan she went on, 'Daddy was the patient.'

'That makes a change, then,' Laura commented. 'What was the problem?'

'His heart,' Josh said.

'Really!' she exclaimed with appropriate concern. 'And what was it that had caused that?'

'It was broken,' the young nurse in charge said, observing them with a look that was old beyond her years.

'We've had to mend it with sticky tape,' Josh explained.

'Incredible!' she breathed.

'Like father, like children,' Gabriel said, smiling at her above their heads, 'You see before you an amazing recovery.' Laura felt as if she was on solid ground for once.

For a moment they were back how they used to be, together, laughing at the antics of their offspring with all the cobwebs of the past scattering on the wind. If Gabriel had been a father not around much before, he was making up for it now and she loved him for it.

When the four of them were seated around the table for their evening meal it was still there, the tranquillity that came with minds in tune, brief though it might turn out to be.

It *was* brief, as it happened. They were watching the children have a last romp before bedtime when the vicar appeared at the side of the hedge that surrounded the garden and called across in the husky voice that had attracted Gabriel's attention, 'May I disturb you good people for a moment?'

'Yes, of course,' Laura told him, and went to greet him with a welcoming smile.

'It is actually your husband that I have come to see,' he said.

'I thought it might be,' she told him with the smile still in place, and when Gabriel joined them she left the two men together and went back to her seat on the patio to avoid being reminded on a tranquil summer night of the uncertainty of Gabriel's future in cancer care.

'I have come to express my gratitude for your concern on my behalf, Dr Armitage,' the vicar said as the two men shook hands. 'It was almost as if you were heaven sent. It seems I do have some cancer of the throat and am being given radiotherapy to see if it will clear up the problem.

'Thanks to you, it has been caught in its early stages and the outlook is good so I am very much indebted to you. Do I take it that you are having a sabbatical from your work here in our lovely village?'

'Er, yes, something like that,' Gabriel told him.

'So where is it that you practise?'

From her seat in the garden Laura couldn't hear the question being asked in the other man's hoarse voice, but she could tell what it was by Gabriel's reply, and it was as if their moments of togetherness earlier had never been as he said, 'I'm not involved with cancer care at the moment. I suppose you could say I'm at a crossroads, undecided which one to travel along in the future.'

'Ah, yes, I see,' the vicar said, and changed the subject as Laura decided it was time that she joined them. 'There is a barn supper in the village hall on Friday night,' he informed them. 'Do come along if you get the chance.'

'Yes, we will,' she told him, and off he went, back to the vicarage and an anxious wife.

'So what is a barn supper?' Gabriel asked when he'd gone

'It is a Country and Western type evening with dancing and a supper that everyone contributes to,' she told him. 'They were talking about it at the practice otherwise I wouldn't be so well informed.'

'I see, and now that you've explained that, Laura, perhaps you can tell me why the shutters are down again between us? Is it what I said to the vicar about the job?'

'It could be,' she told him. 'It sounded so lightweight the way you explained it.'

Lightweight, he thought grimly. It was the first time he'd ever heard a nightmare described as such.

Most of the refurbishment of the surgery had been completed. The building work had been passed by insurers and an outside company connected with the local council, to put Laura's mind and everyone else's at rest, and now it was carpet-fitting time with new seating ready and waiting to be put in position. As the final stages of the project unfolded before her, she wished her life would untangle itself so pleasantly.

There was much progress also taking place on the clinic next to the practice and Libby had once said when the two of them were taking their lunch break together that her father, when next he came to Swallowbrook from his home in Somerset, would be pleased to know that the farm he had neglected all those years ago was bearing fruit of a different sort from what he had grown, in the form of a centre of hope for the sick and suffering.

CHAPTER SIX

IT WOULD be Libby's last day soon and all the staff had been invited to a farewell party that Laura had been asked to arrange on behalf of the practice.

Previous similar occasions had been held at the hotel on the lakeside. John Gallagher, Nathan's father, and one-time head of the practice, had chosen to have his retirement party there, and so had Laura's uncle, Gordon Jessup, who had preceded her as practice manager.

But Libby's choice was one of the launches that sailed the lake with restaurant and bar facilities, and everyone was looking forward to the new venue.

Gabriel had been invited, along with other partners of surgery staff. Josh and Sophie were also on the guest list at Toby's request, and there had been a suggestion that Sophie bring a school friend for company if she wanted to.

With that event to take place shortly, the other three doctors were turning their thoughts to a replacement for Libby, and along with her other duties Laura was arranging interviews to find a suitable candidate.

Her working days seemed to fly past as summer wended its way towards autumn. Having Gabriel there for Sophie and Josh during the long summer holiday from school was solving what could have been a problem otherwise, though not an insurmountable one with holiday clubs available for children with working parents.

But being with their father, who always had something interesting planned for the three of them, was what they liked best, and until they were asleep in the evening after the day's activities everything was fine.

After that, with Gabriel doing jobs in the garden and Laura drawn to what was left of the sun, the feeling of living separate lives was still there.

* * *

The four of them went to the barn supper as Laura had told the vicar they would, and it felt good, Gabriel thought when they arrived, as if they were no longer newcomers to Swallowbrook but belonged there.

As the children went to seek out their friends he took Laura's hand and as they joined the dancers already in Country and Western mood he smiled across at her.

Laura smiled back and it was there again, one of the brief moments of togetherness that came suddenly and went as quickly, but not this time, he hoped. When the caller cried, 'Swing your partner,' he swung her into his arms and held her close, and the longing they had for each other was there, vibrant, demanding, and never brought out into the open since the day that Gabriel had told her he was giving up medicine.

When the dance was over, still holding her hand, he led her onto the deserted village green and in the shadow of an old oak tree that looked as if it had been there for centuries he said, 'When we arrived everyone smiled and waved and I had a fantastic feeling of belonging. It was like coming

home, as if this place had always been waiting for me. Do you have that kind of feeling
about Swallowbrook, Laura?'

'I didn't at first because you weren't
there,' she said. 'I saw the house that my
uncle gave us as just a means to an end with
a job thrown in, and it still feels like that
sometimes because we've lost something
special along the way.'

She saw him flinch. 'But, yes, I do love
living here, the children are so happy away
from the big-city atmosphere and I enjoy
working at the practice. But there are bigger issues at stake, aren't there, Gabriel?'

Watching his face darken, she knew that
it would have been better if she'd let the
matter of his career stay in the background
of their lives, as she'd promised herself she
would, because she'd just spoilt the moment
that had been theirs when they'd left the
dancing and come out into the scented night
to be alone.

'I'm sorry,' she said contritely.

'For what?' he wanted to know. 'Sorry
for what you knew was going to happen the
moment we were out here alone, or sorry for

mentioning the unmentionable—my lack of employment?'

'No, I'm sorry for breaking into the feeling of togetherness that comes so rarely in our lives these days,' she told him. 'I do understand how much you are hurting, but ever since you came back to me from that unmentionable place I've felt that you are shutting me out.'

'That's because I feel so guilty about everything.'

'Yes, I know,' she said gently, and reaching across she held his head between her hands and brushed her lips against his fleetingly, and the moment, delayed by her earlier comment, came surging back, this time with it feeling so right to be in Gabriel's arms with her mouth tender beneath his kisses and her body language telling its own story.

But they weren't exactly in the master bedroom of the house. Any moment someone might come along, and the children were only feet away inside the village hall, so at last he said reluctantly, 'We need to go

back inside. Sophie and Josh will be wondering where we are.'

She nodded, and when she held out her
hand he encircled it with his and they joined
the dancers once more, as if they'd never
been absent.

When it was time for the buffet that everyone had contributed to the vicar was
there, looking less than his usual cherubic
self after his first radiotherapy treatment
but smiling and chatting as best he could to
some of those present, and as he watched
him Gabriel was overwhelmed by a feeling
of uselessness.

Was that all he had to his credit over recent weeks and the months out of circula-
tion? he wondered. His only role to provide
a warning to the unsuspecting that there
might be cause for alarm? He ought to be
doing more than that, much, much more. If
he wasn't carrying the burden of guilt that
had made him tell Laura that his work with
cancer patients was over, he would be back
in the thick of it by now...*if those in authority would let him*.

The vicar's wife was approaching and

knowing that the role of bystander could sometimes be almost as painful as that of the patient, he waited to see what it was that she wanted of him and was not surprised when she said, 'Am I right to be concerned that my husband is doing so much talking after the treatment, Dr Armitage? He is so used to chatting to everyone and thinks he can carry on like that, but...'

'He should be resting his voice as much as possible at the moment,' he told her. 'It will be painful for him to talk. I suggest that you persuade him to go home where he will not feel the need to chat.' He smiled reassuringly for the anxious woman. 'Tell the vicar that is what I advise him to do.'

There was silence as the four of them walked the short distance home after the barn supper. Sophie and Josh were tired after the late night and their parents were thinking their own thoughts.

Laura was remembering Gabriel's conversation with the vicar's wife and thinking he must surely be aware of how little he had to do with oncology in their present situation. For his part, Gabriel's feeling of inadequacy had returned to haunt him.

But the most memorable moments of the evening had been those they'd spent in the shadow of the old oak tree. For a precious short time they'd been moulded into one, like they used to be, and he wondered if she would come to him when the children were asleep to carry on where they'd left off.

Laura had showered and perfumed herself once Sophie and Josh had drifted into dreamland and it was as she was crossing the landing to Gabriel's room that she heard Sophie cry out in pain.

He'd heard it too as the door swung open immediately, and after one startled look in her direction he rushed to where Sophie's cries were becoming louder. Grabbing a robe hung behind the door to cover her scanty nightwear, she followed him at the same speed, with everything else forgotten except their daughter's need of them.

She was crying out in pain, flushed, had a temperature, and her cheeks were wet with tears as Gabriel asked gently, 'What's wrong, Sophie? Where does it hurt, sweet-heart?'

'It's my tummy,' she cried, and as he pulled down the covers Laura saw that her small abdomen was swollen. Gabriel was feeling it gently and when he touched the lower part of it on the right side she cried out and started to sob more loudly.

'Could be appendicitis,' he told Laura, taking her to one side, 'but it is very rare in young children. We need to get Sophie to hospital. Will you go and get Josh up? The three of us need to get dressed fast, but first I'm going to call an ambulance and Josh will have to come with us. There is no one we can disturb at this hour to come and stay with him.'

'She is so young to have something like that,' Laura breathed as she helped a sleepy Josh back into the clothes that he'd only taken off a short time ago. 'Please don't let it be appendicitis.'

Gabriel thought, Please don't let it be any-thing worse, and if it is the appendix let us get there before the pain disappears, which means it's going to burst and she might develop peritonitis.

They were waiting for them in A and E and the doctor they saw was of the same opinion as Gabriel, that it might be appendicitis, but before tests were commenced he asked, 'Has your daughter had a cough or cold in the last few days, or raised lymph glands in the neck?'

'We haven't had cause to think her lymph glands were swollen,' Laura told him, 'but she had a virus sort of thing a week ago.'

'Why do you ask?' Gabriel wanted to know. 'Are you thinking that it might not be appendicitis, that it could be connected with some kind of mesenteric inflammation?'

'It could be,' the doctor replied. 'Do I take it that you are in the medical profession yourself?'

'Yes, I'm an oncologist, so this kind of thing isn't my forte, but I know that mesenteric adenitis is more likely to affect a child than appendicitis and can easily be mistaken for it.'

'Wow! Good for you!' the other man complimented him. 'So let us hope that we are both right, for your little girl's sake, and now we shall do some tests.'

Laura had only been able to take in part of what they were saying as she was comforting Sophie and wiping away Josh's tears, which had been flowing ever since she'd had to wake him with the news that his sister was sick. The only time they had dried up for a few moments had been when he'd been enjoying the novelty of the ride in the ambulance.

She felt like weeping herself. Their beautiful daughter, who she sometimes thought was old beyond her years, was ill with something that could be very serious for a child of her age, and she was just as frightened and vulnerable as any eight-year-old would be in such circumstances.

'What is this thing that it might be?' she asked anxiously of Gabriel as they watched over her while tests were being done.

It was a blessed relief to have him there at such a time and the thought was present that in their lives before Swallowbrook he might have still been operating at that time of night.

'It is an acute disorder caused by lymph nodes in the membrane that keeps the stomach organs attached to the abdominal wall,' he explained. 'It usually occurs in children rather than adults after a throat or chest infection. The pain that comes with it is low on the right side of the abdomen, the same as in appendicitis, so care has to be taken not to confuse the two.'

'And which is the most serious?' she asked frantically.

'Appendicitis. The other usually clears up over a short time with analgesics to relieve the pain, so let's hope that is what it is. We should soon know.'

He took her hand in his. 'Laura, darling, I'm not going to let anything happen to our beautiful daughter, you can trust me on that. If there has to be an operation to remove the appendix I will request that I'm there while it is taking place. But let us not cross our bridges too soon.' He turned to Josh, who was looking tired and woebegone, and said gently, 'Are you watching what the doctors and nurses are doing for when we play that game again?'

'Yes, but it isn't pretend, is it?' Josh said. 'And I don't like it when it isn't.'

Neither do we, Laura thought raggedly, but the doctor in A and E was smiling when the test results came through and he told them, 'It is lymphmesenteric adenitis, to give it its full name. It should quieten down in a few hours with pain relief and rest.

'We want to keep her here for observation for a couple of days just to be on the safe side, but she should be all right after that. It is one of those things that flare up out of nowhere for a child and can be pretty painful at the onset. We are going to transfer Sophie to the children's ward and you can stay with her as long as you like.'

Laura felt that the relief was like healing balm on raw nerve endings as they walked beside the hospital trolley with Sophie on it, now drowsy as the illness began to subside after her being given pain control medication, and as her glance met Gabriel's she couldn't believe that in what seemed like another life she had told him she wanted a divorce. Whether near or far away, he was the centre of her world and always would be.

* * *

This was what their life together could be like if she would let it, Laura thought as she sat watching over Sophie at one side of the bed in the children's ward, with Gabriel sitting opposite and Josh asleep beside her on a visitor's chair.

She could have the relief of always having her husband there when she needed him if he kept to his resolve to give up on the stresses and never-ending demands of an oncologist consultant.

He was holding Sophie's hand and talking to her softly as the pain continued to ease, and she thought that with a nine-to-five position somewhere local he would still be around to walk the children to school, and if home first he could start preparations for the evening meal, and in times like this would be in charge, strong and reliable.

Life could be so good. She loved Swallowbrook and her position at the practice. It had helped to fill the empty days while they had been away from each other, and had given her shattered life some sense of purpose.

But there was one thing that would always prevent the present state of affairs becoming an idyllic kind of life for them all. Gabriel would end up feeling a lesser person because he had turned his back on his patients *and she could not be a party to that!*

The paediatric consultant on his ward rounds in the middle of the morning pronounced Sophie well enough to go home as she was now pain free and sitting up and taking notice of what was going on.

'We would have kept your daughter in for another twenty-four hours if there had been any signs that the infection hadn't cleared,' he told them, 'but she has fought it off very well and hopefully seen the last of it. Obviously bring her back if there is any recurrence of the adenitis, but I'm inclined to think that it was just an isolated incident due to the viral infection she'd had the week before.'

The atmosphere in the house for the rest of the weekend was subdued, with Gabriel in sombre mood, Josh still sleepy after being wakened and transported to A and E in the

middle of the night, and Laura speechless
with relief to know that Sophie wasn't seriously ill.

The only one of them who seemed to
have benefited from the worrying incident
was the patient herself, who, having been in
close contact with real doctors and nurses,
was keen for Josh and herself to take on the
roles again, but was disappointed to find
that having seen them at close range her
brother wasn't all that keen.

On Monday morning it was back to normal-
ity, with Sophie fully recovered, and Laura
left the three excitedly planning how to fill
their day

At the surgery Laura was making final
arrangements with the caterers she had
hired for Libby's farewell party and feeling more like taking a long walk to clear
away the thoughts about Gabriel that had
been going round and round in her head
since Sophie had been taken ill.

When Ruby came to her office in the
middle of the morning and asked if she'd
had a good weekend she was greeted with

a definite 'No!' and it was therapeutic to be able to tell the slender young doctor about Sophie's brief but frightening illness.

'I've never heard of that before,' Ruby said when Laura described it.

'Neither had I,' Laura told her, 'but Gabriel had, needless to say.' And when Ruby had gone back to her patients Laura allowed her thoughts to go back to the moment on the landing when she'd been going to Gabriel to make up for all the times they'd slept separately.

He would have known what she'd had in mind after seeing her outside his bedroom door, but hadn't mentioned it since then and neither had she. Sophie's illness had blotted out everything else with the frightening speed with which it had come on. Sophie had been their first priority, and the moment of the rekindling of their passion hadn't materialised.

Gabriel called in during the lunch hour, minus the children, who were on play dates, to check that she was all right after the upsets of the weekend, and with the memory clear of him finding her outside his bedroom door her colour began to rise, yet why, for goodness' sake? He'd seen her like that often enough before the day that had put a dividing line between them that had proved to be so hard to cross.

She wasn't to know that his thoughts had been running along the same lines. He was totally relieved to have been there for Sophie when she'd needed his love and his medical expertise, but for the rest of it he couldn't believe that Laura had been coming to him for the first time in months at the very second that they'd heard her cry out.

So where did they go from here? Certainly not jumping into bed as if there wasn't a moment to spare, that was for certain. He had waited a long time for Laura to come to him and could wait longer if he had to.

A replacement for Libby had been found and was due to join the practice in a few weeks' time. Aaron Somerton, in his late thirties, was an acquaintance of Nathan's from when he had worked in a hospital in Africa for three years before coming back to Swallowbrook and discovering that his life belonged here with Libby.

Aaron occasionally rang for a chat and when he'd phoned one night to say that he was coming back to the UK and was looking for a less stressful life for a while, Nathan had mentioned the upcoming vacancy in the practice and Aaron had been immediately interested.

Having experience of the other man's worth from the time they'd worked together previously, Nathan had suggested that, subject to the agreement of the other doctors, he should join the practice for a trial period, and arrangements were now moving in that direction.

Aaron was unmarried and Laura at his request was in the process of finding him somewhere to live.

A couple of choices were available and she was on her way to view them one afternoon the following week when she met Gabriel with a line and rod that her uncle had left behind when he'd gone to live in Spain.

The children had been invited to the birthday party of one of their school friends and he was taking the opportunity to spend a peaceful afternoon on the bank of a nearby river.

'Hi. Where are you off to?' he enquired.

'I'm house-hunting,' she told him.

'Really! Who for?'

'The new doctor, Libby's replacement,' she explained, feeling suddenly irritated. At one time she would have been delighted to find him relaxing on a summer afternoon, but not now. It was as if he was going from one extreme to the other, that the role of overworked oncologist was being replaced by that of the local layabout, and when he flashed her a smile, not having immediately tuned in to her cooling-off, she said, without considering the effect it might have on him, 'How can you idle the time away like this, Gabriel, like some sort of layabout, when there are so many who need you?'

The smile disappeared. 'It would seem that we are at cross-purposes once again,' he said levelly. 'I've been trying to make up for past mistakes but I'm still not getting it right, am I? What exactly is it that you want of me, Laura?'

She was about to tell him that she wanted
it to be the same as before, with him treating
the sick with the degree of fulfilment that it
had always brought but with a smaller workload, *not giving up medicine altogether!*

But the word *layabout* hung on the air
like judgement from above.

How could she have been so cruel as to
say such a thing? She wanted to tell him
how sorry she was, but he wasn't giving her
the chance. Gabriel was striding off towards
the river as if there was nothing more to be
said, and moving off in the opposite direction she began the task of finding a place
to live for the stranger who would soon be
in their midst.

After viewing the two properties that
she'd narrowed the choice down to Laura
decided on a spacious cottage up for rental
with views of the lake and fells, and once
back in her office emailed the details to
Aaron Somerton and awaited his comments.

When she arrived home at the end of what
had been a miserable day there was the
smell of fish cooking and she wondered if

it was Gabriel's reply to the way she'd described him. He'd caught a salmon, she discovered when she bent to peep inside the oven, and it looked delicious.

As she was straightening up, his voice came from behind, and as if their earlier exchange of words had been without rancour he said easily, 'Not bad for a layabout, eh, Laura?' and went on to explain, 'I met John Gallagher, Nathan's father, while I was down there. He lives in one of those delightful pine lodges by the river, and as I wasn't aware that I needed a permit to fish there he said that if questioned I could use his, which explains our colourful friend in the oven.'

'You never cease to amaze me,' she said laughingly.

'And disappoint you equally?' he questioned.

'No, never that,' she protested. 'All I ever want for you is the best out of life, Gabriel.

'I've got it. You and the children are that.'

'Maybe we are to some extent, but you deserve more, and I won't go into the details of that as you are already aware of them and must be weary of my frequent reminders.'

As the smell of the salmon strengthened and vegetables on the hotplate came to the boil she said in a lighter tone, 'So, are you going to open a bottle of wine to celebrate your first catch?'

'Yes, why not?' he agreed. 'And there are plenty of cold drinks for the children.'

'So I'll go up and get changed,' she said, the day's pressures lifting. 'I don't want my surgery clothes to smell of a fisherman's catch.'

'Some fisherman, though!' he said, with eyes warming, and he swung her into his arms and danced her up the stairs to where the children were playing in their bedrooms, and when they came out onto the landing to see what all the noise was about and found her laughing up at him, she said, 'We never get the timing right, do we?'

'No, but we will,' he promised, and she so wanted to believe him.

Where had all Gabriel's good humour come from though? Only that afternoon there had been coolness between them when she'd referred to him as a layabout. Surely catching the salmon wasn't the reason for his light-heartedness?

Yet it seemed as if it might be as while they were eating it he said, 'Nathan's father reckoned the salmon was one of the biggest catches for months down on the river, *and from an amateur.*'

He didn't explain that his good humour came from knowing that.

James had phoned to say that the hearing before the hospital board in London had been given a date, and much as he, Gabriel, wouldn't be looking forward to it, he saw it as one of two things—a new beginning or an ending. Once that had been decided he could sort out his working life. It was to take place in a month's time and he would be marking off the days to it.

He was going to break the news to Laura when the children were in bed and knew it would blow away the happiness of the day, but she had to know and would not take kindly to any delay in the telling of it.

'So it has come at last,' she said when he'd told her about the phone call, and she'd thought that the timing wasn't good, today of all days when they were so happy, but when would be a good moment to pass on that sort of news?

She understood Gabriel's relief to have heard something definite from the London end, but felt sick inside at the thought what it might mean.

'I'll go with you when the time comes,' she told him, but he shook his head.

'No way,' he told her. 'I caused the situation and I will sort it one way or the other, and until then, Laura, let's put it out of our minds and carry on enjoying life in Swallowbrook.'

'Do you think we can?' she whispered

'I'm sure we can,' he told her, 'and if we can hang on long enough, let's save that special moment that keeps eluding us until I come back from the hearing. If the news is good it will be a celebration and if it's bad it will be a sign of our strength. Yes?'

'Yes,' she agreed, and had never loved him more than she did then.

CHAPTER SEVEN

WHEN Laura arrived at the practice there was a message from Aaron Somerton to say that the cottage looked delightful, and asking her to put a hold on it for him. The message went on to say that he would be joining them in late September, would not expect to be met, and would make his way to Swallowbrook straight from the airport, as he did have some knowledge of the area.

So much for that, she thought. He was obviously someone who liked to have his finger on the pulse in more ways than one.

When Gabriel had told her about the phone call from James the night before she'd been amazed that he was so happy and cheerful knowing that the ordeal he had to face would soon be upon him.

'It would suit me if it was tomorrow,' he'd told her. 'I want to get it over with. It has been hanging over me like a black cloud and whatever the outcome at least I will know then what choices I have.'

He would be going back to be judged in the place where he'd saved so many lives and prolonged others, but not in recent months, he'd thought as he and the children had waved Laura off that morning with an arrangement that they would meet her for lunch.

He carried a burden of blame for having been absent from those who needed him, and without saying it out loud, if it hadn't been that he'd let someone else down too, he would have been pushing to get back in there long ago.

He knew Laura wouldn't have slept much after discovering that a day had been set for the hearing and had thought that a meal at the nearest of the restaurants would be better than a quick sandwich, so when she came out of the practice building the three of them were waiting for her, one on either side of him, holding his hand, and she turned away so that he wouldn't see tears on her lashes.

Gabriel's only crime had been caring too much about the sick who came to him, always being there for them, giving them the benefit of every ounce of his expertise, and he was still paying for it, she thought sadly.

. Since he'd been back with her and the children he'd done everything in his power to make things right between them, even offering to cut himself off from his work if it would make her happier, with never a complaint about being shut away because a moment of righteous anger had turned into something else.

She knew he was tuning in to her thoughts as he watched her fight back the tears, but he made no comment. Instead he said, 'Let's go, Laura, or your lunch hour will be over before you've had time to eat.' And the four of them began to move in the direction of the nearest restaurant on the lakeside.

There was a garden at the back with tables and chairs and for a precious short time Laura felt at peace with herself as the four of them sat in a leafy arbour enjoying their lunch.

Until Sophie said, out of the blue, 'I don't want to live in our other house again. I want to stay here for always, but if we sell it, where will Daddy sleep when he goes back to work in London?'

As Laura waited to see what the reply to that would be he said, 'On a park bench, I suppose. Or I could stay with Uncle James maybe.'

No mention of him not going back to work in London, she noted, so what was that supposed to mean? That Gabriel had changed his mind about giving up medicine, but wasn't going to admit it in case he wasn't allowed to go back? Was it another decision that she wasn't going to be consulted about?

As the days passed Libby's farewell party was something special to look forward to and with that thought in mind Laura took Sophie shopping for dresses on the Saturday after the phone call from James with the date of the hearing.

'What colour shall I wear?' she asked Gabriel before they set off.

'You always look stunning in black,' was his reply.

'And me?' Sophie wanted to know.

'How about yellow or blue for my beautiful daughter?' he said, and Laura thought if he'd suggested all the colours of the rainbow Sophie would have been happy if they'd been her father's choice.

It was lovely to see them together. She had been so unhappy while he'd been away from them, unable to understand why he hadn't been there, and no way had she been going to tell her where he was as Sophie would have been bewildered and upset.

They shopped for her first, and at Gabriel's suggestion chose a pretty party dress in pale yellow that was perfect to go with her dark hair and eyes. Then it was her own turn to find something and she settled on a black cocktail dress because she needed to be told she looked stunning, that she wasn't the miserable drab that she felt most of the time, and Gabriel was the only one she wanted to hear it from.

* * *

But before she was to hear those words from her husband there was a surprising announcement from Ruby and Hugo. Laura had invited them round for supper one night and when the children were in bed and the four of them were sitting in the garden Hugo said to his new wife, 'Are we going to tell Laura and Gabriel our good news, Ruby?'

They are going to announce that Ruby is pregnant, Laura thought. These two delightful people are going to cement their marriage with a child.

But as Ruby explained with heightened colour exactly what their good news was, she realised that though a child was involved it wouldn't be theirs. They had been accepted on to the waiting list of adoptive parents and some time in the future would be given the chance to adopt.

Before arriving that evening they had discussed sharing their problem with Laura and Gabriel in confidence, knowing that they could rely on them not to spread around the reason why they couldn't have children of their own.

Taking Ruby's hand in his, Hugo explained,

'We could have children of our own, lots of them if we wanted, but they could be born with the same gene that Ruby carries, that of haemophilia, which could give any boy children we might have the blood-clotting problem and any girls the burden of being a carrier.

'Neither of us would want to wish that on to any child of ours, so we will either foster or adopt when we are ready, and would ask that you keep this matter to yourselves, if you don't mind.'

'Of course,' Gabriel said, and Laura, holding Ruby close like she would a younger sister, wiped a tear from her eye as she thought that sometimes the troubles of others helped to bring one's own nightmares into perspective.

When they'd gone Gabriel said, 'Those two are something special, aren't they?'

'Yes, they really are,' she agreed. 'Nathan did the same kind of thing, adopted Toby when both his parents were killed in a ferry disaster while they were on holiday. He was saved, and Nathan, who was his godfather, went out to get him, and as there were no close relatives to take him he adopted him and arrived back in Swallowbrook as a single father.'

'Hugo is fantastic with children. Nearly all parents with a sick child who come to the surgery ask to see Dr Lawrence. He would have made a wonderful father to any children they might have had, but it would seem that he is prepared to forego that because he loves Ruby so much, and you have to hand it to them, they are going to do the next best thing.'

He nodded sombrely. What *he* was thinking of doing could be described as the next best thing and time was pressing. He'd promised James that he would be in touch but it wasn't that simple. There was another side to it that he had to sort and he needed to do that first.

The following morning Ruby sought Laura out in her office, as she sometimes did, for a brief chat and the first thing she said was, 'When would you be free for us to return your hospitality, Laura? Either at the weekend or an evening during the week, either time would be all right for us.

'I know that the coming weekend is going to be stressful for you, having to oversee Libby's farewell party, so will leave it with you when you are able to come. Just say the word when you are free.'

As she was about to go back upstairs she hesitated in the doorway and asked, 'What did you think about me not being able to give Hugo the children that he would love to have?'

'I thought that you were two amazing people with a love for each other that is strong and true,' she told her, 'and so did Gabriel. Ruby, you have only to look at Libby and Nathan with Toby to know that what you and Hugo are planning to do in the future for some parentless child or children will be a wonderful thing for all of you.'

'I needed to hear that,' she said. 'Sometimes it just gets to me that I can't give the man I love children of his and my blood because mine is tainted, but he won't hear of it when I tell him how sorry I am, and every now and then I need someone to say the things that you have just said to me. Thanks for that, Laura.'

Ruby was smiling as she went to join Hugo at the start of the weekly antenatal clinic that the two of them staffed, and Laura thought that to the rare woman with a problem like that of Ruby, the monitoring of someone else's foetus must be a bitter pill to swallow, but the young doctor who had just gone to do that very thing had an unselfishness that would carry her through whatever had to be done.

She was sure that if Ruby had asked the other doctors to be spared that part of her duties they would have understood, but with Hugo's love and her own acceptance of the blight that a hereditary gene had put upon her, she would cope.

The clinic beside the practice was taking shape from every angle. Soon it would be open and ready to take some of the burden off the main cancer unit at the hospital on the lakeside, and every time Laura gazed at its immaculate newness it brought a lump to her throat to know that someone would be doing the job that Gabriel excelled at within its walls, while he went fishing.

At the practice she was finalising the arrangements for the party and with that and her other normal duties the days seemed to be flying past.

All the surgery staff would be there to say farewell to the doctor who had spent all her working life looking after the health of Swallowbrook and its surrounding hamlets and was now about to take on the full-time role of motherhood.

There would be music and dancing on board, a buffet and a bar, and at some time during the evening elderly John Gallagher, who had been head of the practice when Libby had come straight from university to work there, and was now her father-in-law, would make the presentation that everyone had contributed to.

If Laura had been less busy she would have realised that Gabriel was preoccupied, and might have been surprised at him leaving the house one evening without explanation, but she'd reasoned that he was around the place all day with the children, so it wasn't surprising that he felt the need for a change of scene.

It would soon be a year to the day since she had appeared in his consulting room as a patient, and it would be an anniversary of pain and horror that would never go away until their lives were back on track.

But she'd given up on that, had accepted that second best was going to have to do. If she had to live with the knowledge that his days of cancer care were over it would be her punishment for wanting more from him than he'd had the time or energy to give.

He'd returned a couple of hours later looking calm enough, but hadn't lingered to talk. Instead, he'd just patted her cheek and gone straight to bed.

The night of the party on the boat was clear and starless with just a pale harvest moon in the sky, and as Laura watched Libby in the last stages of pregnancy greet her guests she was positioned nearby to make sure the arrangements she'd made were being carried out satisfactorily.

She'd gone ahead to be there from the start, leaving Gabriel and the children to follow, and as she watched the guests arriving she saw them walking along the landing stage towards her.

Sophie had on the new yellow dress as she held her friend Lily's hand, Josh was in long trousers and a smart short-sleeved shirt, and Gabriel was wearing a white dinner jacket, black trousers and bow-tie, and as she watched him approach Laura was aware of heads turning at the sight of the practice manager's husband.

Whether they were thinking the same as she was, that he would be the most attractive man there, or if he was of interest because it was said he'd been in prison, she didn't know, as some of the guests weren't the surgery staff who knew the story. They were relations and friends of Libby and Nathan.

Yet did she care what people thought? She was wearing the black dress that she'd bought to please him and knew he'd been right. The black *did* show off her golden fairness, and as he looked up at her from beneath the floodlights that were all around the boat it was there, the question that she sometimes saw in his eyes. *Do you still love me, Laura?* And she wondered how he could ever doubt it.

They didn't sleep together, admittedly, but Gabriel had been the one to reject *her* first, when she'd been longing to have him beside her again in the long night hours after he'd served his sentence, but instead he'd gone straight to the London house.

And even when he had come to Swallowbrook he had set a precedent that first night by sleeping in the spare room. Hurt and angry, she'd gone along with it and now *she* was the one who was choosing to sleep alone and wondering how long she could stand the loneliness of it.

The two of them talked more about surface things than what really mattered, yet she was there, wasn't she, ready and willing to accept a life of lesser closeness if he would only open up to her.

When they stepped onto the deck beside her Gabriel bent and kissed her meaningfully and when he put her away from him

Laura saw a glint in the dark eyes looking down at her.

'That was for the benefit of those who have been sizing me up,' he said in a low voice as a waiter approached with a tray of drinks, and after passing glasses of fruit juice to the children he took champagne for himself when Laura indicated that she wasn't drinking while she was on duty.

The caterers were about to depart before the boat set sail and leaving Gabriel and the three children for a moment she went to thank them for their efforts. When she turned to rejoin them it seemed that Sophie, Josh and Sophie's friend Lily had already found Toby, and Ruby and Hugo had joined Gabriel, which left her free to make sure that all her other arrangements were up to the standard of the catering.

After the presentation had been made and most of the food eaten, Libby said, 'Laura, go and join your family and relax. There is nothing else that you need concern yourself about.'

Maybe not about the party, she thought, but her concerns about the future were many, though it wasn't the moment to be worrying about that, so she said, 'Yes, I will if you don't mind. Gabriel was with Ruby and Hugo, but I think they've met up with friends and he doesn't know many people here.'

Gabriel was leaning against the rail of the boat with arms folded when she found him, staring down thoughtfully at the foaming backwash that it was creating as it ploughed slowly through the water, and when she tucked her arm in his he straightened up and asked, 'Is that it, the finish of a job well done?'

'More or less,' she replied, and thought that Libby must surely be thinking along those lines as she said goodbye to the practice that she'd served so faithfully.

Looking around her, she asked, 'Where are the children?'

'They're on the lower deck, playing games with the other young ones on board,' he told her. He looked around him at the rest of the party guests. 'Now can I get you a drink?'

'Yes, please,' she said thankfully, and as

she watched him stride off towards the bar thought achingly that her husband was a man amongst men, compassionate, caring, clever, and *for once in his life so unsure of himself that he couldn't or wouldn't talk to her about it.*

The magical sail across the long length of the lake and back was over. The party guests were making their way home, but the first stop for Laura and Gabriel was at the farm where Sophie's friend Lily lived, and once she had been safely delivered to her parents he drove them the short distance to Swallows Barn with Josh already asleep in the back seat of the car.

Scooping him up into his arms, Gabriel carried him inside and deposited him just as he was onto his bed and then drew the covers over him, and as Laura helped a tired Sophie to undress and then disappeared into her own room, silence descended on the house.

They were all tired except him, Gabriel thought, going out to sit in the moonlit garden. He felt restless and on edge as he thought of Laura sleeping above after a task completed to her satisfaction.

It was clear that she'd found the right sort of niche in the job at the practice and was able to see the results of her efforts the same as it had once been for him, and he couldn't go on much longer as the 'layabout' she'd described him as in a moment of frustration.

His life now was what he'd sometimes yearned for during the long and taxing days on the unit, yet its appeal was dwindling. He loved being with Laura and the children, but something had to give. He couldn't hold back any longer.

The energy he'd always had was back, the urge to heal and make well again was there once more, and so was Laura, who'd been hurt and ignored, and would be hurt again, beyond belief, if she was ever made to feel that she was the stumbling block that was keeping him from his patients.

A light footstep behind him and she was there, dressed in a crumpled nightdress, rubbing the sleep out of her eyes. When he gazed at her in surprise she said thickly, 'I went into your room. You weren't there and it all came back! The nights when I wandered around knowing that you were somewhere else, in a strange place, far away from us. So I had to come and find you, to make sure that you were actually here, that I wasn't dreaming.'

She was swaying with tiredness and was turning to go back to bed now that she'd satisfied herself that he was there, where she could see him.

'Of course I'm here, Laura. Where else would I be?' he said gently, and even as he said it a vision of the operating theatre where he'd spent so many hours came back to plague him.

He swept her up into his arms and she lay there limply as he carried her up the stairs with the same gentleness that he'd shown to Josh earlier. After laying her carefully between the covers he sat beside her and held her hand until she was soundly asleep once more, and then went across the landing and opened his bedroom door wide, so that if she should awake again with the same feeling of dread she would be able to see him not far away.

* * *

His unexplained absence on the night when he'd left the house and not said where he was going had been because he'd had a phone call from Nathan during the day while Laura was at the practice. It had been about something they'd discussed a few times but hadn't yet brought to a conclusion, though not for the want of trying, and he had told Nathan that he would call round that evening.

When they'd finished talking, and he was leaving Nathan and Libby's extended cottage across the way from the surgery he'd said, 'I would be obliged if you didn't say anything about this to Laura in case nothing comes of it, Nathan. I've caused her enough distress already and don't want her to feel that I've messed up our lives once again if it turns out to be a letdown.'

As he'd gone striding off Nathan had thought that there went a man who had been to hell and back because of doing the job he excelled at to the extreme. He had paid a heavy price because of it, and there weren't many like him around.

Gabriel had come away from their chat

feeling optimistic about the future, that if they gave him the go-ahead at the hearing he was going to be able to get it sorted soon in all their best interests.

But now, after seeing Laura's distress when she'd dreamt that she was back in the days of his imprisonment, he decided that tomorrow he would wait to see if she mentioned the bad dream.

It could have been that her mind had been on overdrive after the pressures of being responsible for the party arrangements. She'd been down by the lake most of the day and had been exhausted by the time they'd arrived home.

It was a long time before he fell into a restless sleep when he went up to bed, and his first thoughts on waking were of when she'd appeared in such distress and let down her guard about the bad times of when he'd been taken from them.

As he raised himself up off the pillows he saw that her door was open as he'd left it the night before in case she had a repetition of the bad dream, but the bed was empty and there was no sound of her in the *en suite*.

Without dressing, he went down the stairs at speed and she was there, in the kitchen. The table was set, cereal dishes were laid out, and she was at the cooker, grilling bacon.

When she saw him she came across to where he was standing in the doorway and, reaching up, touched his face gently. 'I'm sorry about last night, Gabriel,' she said. 'I think I'd rather overdone it at the party and although I'd gone straight to sleep, my brain hadn't.'

'Has that sort of thing ever happened before?' he asked carefully.

'No! Last night was just a one-off, a bad dream. Why, what did you think it was?'

'I didn't know, but it did occur to me that it might be something else that I'm responsible for.'

'Don't say things like that!' she cried. 'All you ever did wrong was work too hard. If I could turn back the clock, I would. You aren't the only one to blame for what happened. Our lives will never be right again until we can put the past behind us.'

'Yes, I do know that,' he said gently, and thought that he was the one with the most past to put behind him. Would he ever forget the smells, the bars on the windows and the claustrophobic atmosphere of the place?

The bacon was beginning to sizzle and splutter. It took over the moment and nothing further was said.

On a continent far away Aaron Somerton was preparing to leave the place that had been his home for the last four years and it was a strange feeling to know that he would soon be back on English soil again.

He had been one of the doctors from the UK working at the hospital in an African township when Nathan Gallagher had arrived on a three-year contract, and when it had been up twelve months ago Aaron had been loath to see the other man go, as on meeting they'd discovered that they both came from the same county in England and had been brought up only miles apart.

It was the reason why Aaron had been keen to take Nathan up on his suggestion that he take up temporary employment in the practice at Swallowbrook when he came back to the UK until he had sorted out his future.

The details of the accommodation he'd been sent had caused him to start counting the days and now there were not many left to cross off before he took a flight homewards.

As the two of them had chatted he'd been surprised to hear that Nathan was now married, had adopted a child, and was about to have a child of his own from his new wife, all in the space of a year.

Obviously his ex-colleague was not someone to hesitate when the moment was right, he thought, which wasn't exactly how he would describe himself, and wondered if all those of his kind who came to Africa to work had left behind some unfinished business.

It seemed strange on Monday morning for Libby's consulting room to be empty. Nathan had suggested to Ruby that she move into it as hers was rather small, but she'd told him that she was happy enough where she was, and when he'd reminded her that now she was the only woman doctor in the practice and that she would be getting the bulk of the patients of her own sex, she'd smiled and said, 'Lucky me,' and had meant it, even though there would be many pregnancies amongst them.

Her haemophilia nightmare had become bearable with Hugo surrounding her with his love and tender care and she was happier now than she'd ever been.

In her office in the basement Laura was receiving brief visits from surgery staff wanting to say their bit about how they'd enjoyed Saturday night, and she thought in a moment of quiet that the next happy event in the life of the head of the practice would be the birth of his child.

With sudden yearning the thought came that she and Gabriel could do with a 'happy event'. She would settle for a break in the sun somewhere, far away from painful memories, but they'd let the school's long summer holiday go by.

The next time the children were off would be the October half-term, so why not then? She was due some holiday leave from the

practice, but Gabriel had one big commitment, his appearance before the hospital
board. So it would be better for that to be
over and done with and a holiday would be
just the thing to take away the taste of it.

To her dismay, he didn't show much interest in the idea when she suggested it. His
comment was a lukewarm 'Yes, possibly we
could have a break, but shall we wait until
nearer the time?'

He was taking into account that holidays
meant being together non-stop, she decided.
They would be much closer than in their
daily lives and perhaps in the present state
of their relationship he didn't want to rush
that as he hadn't followed up her proposed
nocturnal visit that had backfired when Sophie had been taken ill.

He had turned away to hide a smile at
her suggestion. It was her birthday in the
middle of October. He'd arranged for the
four of them to go to one of the Greek is-
lands for the week of the school half-term
to celebrate the occasion, and was hoping
that by then he would be able to offer Laura

the peace of mind that he so much wanted
to give her, which all fitted in with his lukewarm response.

CHAPTER EIGHT

IT WAS busy at the practice with a doctor short now that Libby had left.

Laura suggested to Nathan and Hugo that they take on a locum until Aaron Somerton arrived, but as it was only a few weeks until he put in an appearance they decided that it was hardly worth it, and that as the room that had always been Libby's was being decorated ready for his arrival it would be difficult to accommodate a locum.

Those were the problems of her working life, Laura thought, surmountable, possible to sort out. Her home life was a different thing. Every time she thought about the hearing all the new closeness that she and Gabriel had been achieving seemed to diminish, become distant, and she couldn't bear the thought of them going back to how they'd been before.

He hadn't been out in the evening again without explanation but she'd discovered from a casual comment by one of the practice nurses that she'd seen him at the local garage getting fuel one morning and she'd described him as looking 'scrumptious' in a dark suit, white shirt, and tie.

Thinking back, Laura recalled that when she'd arrived home that day Gabriel had been in jeans and a sweatshirt, mowing the lawns, and no comment had been forthcoming about where he'd been off to that morning.

They'd been used to telling each other everything before their breakdown of communications and had made every decision of importance together, but not any more. It wasn't surprising that he was not falling over himself to go on holiday with her. Closer they might be, yet the feeling of being on the fringe of what was happening in Gabriel's life was still there.

She would have been surprised to know that as he had driven out of the village on the appointment that he'd dressed so smartly for, he had been having similar thoughts. Hating to keep things from her but wary of telling her what he was planning in case it all fell apart.

While the children were playing with friends it had seemed that he'd also gone fishing on the day when the nurse had seen him. When Laura had gone into the kitchen to sort out the evening meal his catch had been there, gutted, cleaned and ready for cooking.

For a moment she'd thought that the nurse must have been wrong,

Yet who would mistake the man she was married to, especially in a smart suit, and if that *was* the case, where had he been going?

He'd been his usual self during the evening and the same the next morning at breakfast, but the thought kept niggling at the back of her mind and was still there as she walked the short distance to the practice. They didn't sleep together, didn't talk all that much, he didn't want to holiday with her and went out on secret appointments. How much longer could she cope with this kind of life? she wondered. Roll on the day of the hearing.

There had been a fire at the cricket ground at the opposite end of the village from where the practice was situated. A store-room where equipment was kept had gone up in flames from an electrical fault, to the dismay of the cricketers both old and young, especially the young, who flocked there on weeknights for practice and the opportunity of being with their own age group instead of hanging about on street corners.

Since the catastrophe various fundrais-ing efforts had been held with a view to re-placing what had been lost, and on a night soon to come the Swallowbrook Commu-nity Committee was holding a big barbeque on a field opposite the cricket ground as the final fundraising event. Most of the money had been raised and soon the crick-eters would be back on the pitch with new equipment.

It was to take place on the Saturday night two weeks after Libby's farewell party and Gabriel was keen for them to go because he said that soon Josh and Toby would be there on summer nights with the young throng of hopefuls and maybe even Sophie, as it wasn't unheard of for the girls of the village to turn up for practice.

Laura agreed that whatever the future of the cricket team, the present was calling for their support and bought four tickets for the barbeque from the post office with the thought in mind that if she and Gabriel rarely spent time together with just the two of them, a family outing was always something to treasure.

There were sideshows at one end of the cricket ground with the barbeque positioned opposite, and already there were lots of folk there, mostly villagers with just a few strange faces amongst them.

When they came across Hugo and Ruby he had just won a cocoanut and on seeing his young wife eating candy floss Sophie asked if she could have some, and Gabriel went for it to a stall further down the field.

Laura chatted for a while to the newlyweds with the children playing nearby, and

when they'd moved on she glanced in the direction that Gabriel had taken and saw him
in conversation with the same nurse who
had described him as 'scrumptious' when
she'd seen him at the petrol pumps that day.

She was a captivating creature herself
with long dark hair, hazel eyes with long
lashes, totally beguiling, and whatever she
was saying to Gabriel she certainly had his
full attention. Yet he didn't linger, aware
of Sophie waiting for the candy floss, and
when he joined them again he said thoughtfully, 'That was a nurse from the practice.'

'Yes, I know,' she told him. 'What did
she want?'

'She was asking if the new doctor at the
practice was going to be me, and when I
said no, that it was going to be this Somerton guy, I thought she was going to collapse.
The colour just drained from her face. What
do you think of that?'

'It seems very odd,' she replied. 'Her
name is Julianne Marshall and if I remember rightly I have her address on file at the
surgery as an apartment above the beauty

salon on the main street of the village. Do you think she knows our new doc?'

'Maybe Somerton is from these parts and the name rang a bell,' he commented, and they left it at that and went to see what was happening on the cricket field.

When they arrived back at the house there was a message on the answering-machine to say that her uncle was spending what he described as a 'culture break' in London and would be coming to stay with them overnight the following day.

As she listened to the message from her only relative Laura was filled with a mixture of pleasure and dismay. Pleasure because she was fond of the elderly bachelor who had kept in touch ever since she'd lost both her parents when in her early twenties. Her dismay at the thought of him visiting was smaller than the pleasure, but was there nevertheless because of the situation between Gabriel and herself. He'd gone to live in Spain thinking that once they'd settled in the village it would be the end of their troubles, but her uncle was nobody's fool, *and there was the question of the sleeping arrangements.*

When she relayed the message to Gabriel he smiled. 'That is good. It will be great to see the old guy again, though I suppose you are concerned about where he's going to sleep as I'm using the spare room. Yes?'

'Yes, I am,' she said levelly. There was no way she wanted them to sleep together again under those sorts of circumstances.

'It won't be a problem, Laura,' he told her. 'With a sheet and an extra duvet in your room I'll be fine. Your uncle won't know what the arrangements are once the door is closed behind us. The farce will be for us alone to concern ourselves about.'

Fixing him with a steady blue gaze, she said, 'You always were good at finding the right word when you wanted to describe something, Gabriel, and you still are. A farce is a sham, an empty thing, and if that doesn't describe what our love life has become I can't think what does.' And without giving him the chance to reply, she went to check that the children were asleep before going to bed herself.

He made to follow her, wanting to hold her close and put an end to the thing that was keeping them apart, but what would he have to tell her? Nothing definite, that was for sure, and until there was he would have to wait until the time was right, and it wasn't now.

It was Saturday morning so they were all able to meet Gordon at the local railway station.

When he stepped out onto the platform Laura and Gabriel exchanged smiles. Dressed in a lightweight beige suit with a straw panama hat on his grizzled head, he was the picture of the elderly British ex-pat, and then Laura was hugging him, Gabriel shaking him by the hand, and the children, standing to one side, were warily observing the strange-looking visitor that they didn't see very often.

When they arrived at the house her uncle looked around him at the improvements she'd made. 'This place used to be just somewhere to eat and sleep when I had it. I can't believe it's the same house,' he said approvingly. 'It was always too big for me,

a family like you folks was what it needed.'
His glance still taking in the changes she'd
made, he went on, 'I see that you've had it
re-thatched and whoever did it made a better job of it than before.'

They had lunch on the patio and when
Laura and her uncle were chatting afterwards Gordon said, 'I rang Nathan and his
father while I was on the train to see if some
of us could meet up somewhere tonight and
took the liberty of asking them to come
here, Laura. Is that all right?'

'Yes, of course. It is still just as much
your house as it is ours,' she told him, with
her glance on Gabriel who had gone to the
bottom of the garden to get the children's
ball out of thick bushes where it had just
landed.

'Has the dust of the dreadful thing that
happened to you both settled down?' he
asked in a low voice.

'We're getting there,' she said lightly, and
wished she was a better liar.

'That's good, though I do think you look
a bit peaky,' he commented. His gaze trans-

ferred to Gabriel. 'And your man down there, how is he?'

She had a sudden urge to be truthful instead of doing a cover-up and told him, 'He has changed, compared to how he used to be, not with the children, he is lovely with them the same as he's always been, but Gabriel doesn't share things with me like he used to.

'He's waiting to go before the hospital board to see if they will agree to him still practising there, but even if they do I'm not sure that he will go back, and I feel so guilty because I was the one who triggered everything off that day. But please don't tell him that I've told you.'

He nodded. 'I promise I won't say a word. Give him time, Laura, that is what he needs.'

'Yes, but how much?' she said. 'He spends his days taking care of the children, going fishing, and is secretive about anywhere else he goes. It is Gabriel that I'm describing, yet it feels like a stranger.'

The evening was a happy one with those who had known each other a long time enjoying the company of old friends they could chat with about times gone by.

Libby and Nathan had come to Swallows Barn to meet up with Gordon once again. John Gallagher was there, eager to chat with someone who had been employed at the practice when he'd been in charge, and although Gordon had only known Hugo and Ruby briefly before he'd left, Laura had invited them because she was fond of Ruby, and her charming husband had been kind and helpful when she'd been moving into the house on her own when Gabriel hadn't been there for her and the children.

When the guests had gone Gordon said, 'I will be off first thing in the morning as I'm having afternoon tea with an old school friend, and have got a ticket for a concert in the evening. I've been doing the rounds of the shows while I've been in London and some sightseeing of special places. It has been exactly how I wanted it to be, a pleasant "culture break".

'I'm off back to Spain on Monday to tie up a few loose ends and shut up my house there for a while.' He observed them both calmly. 'I've been diagnosed with cancer of the prostate and want to be treated over here by you, Gabriel, if you will do that for me.'

There was a shocked silence for a few seconds as they took in what he'd just told them then Gabriel said, 'How long since you found out, Gordon?'

'The doctors over there have been monitoring my prostate count for some time and recently it has shot up quite alarmingly and the diagnosis is cancer.'

'I see, and, yes, it goes without saying that I will take you on as a patient,' Gabriel told him. 'It will be a privilege. Laura has perhaps told you that I haven't gone back to my London clinic, but there are ways and means in which I can treat you privately and be in contact with them at the same time with regard to your treatment if that would be all right with you?'

'And you must stay here with us until you are well again,' Laura said anxiously.

Gordon was smiling, the only one of the three of them who was.

'My answer to your offer, Gabriel, is, yes,

please,' he said, 'and to yours, Laura, no, but thank you just the same. I have taken a rented apartment in London and will stay there during my treatment. I shall go back to Spain whenever possible as it's only a couple of hours' flight and will commute between the two countries.'

'Leave me the details of your medical people over there,' Gabriel told him, 'and I will get on to them to let me have your records and the results of any tests that you've already had sent to me immediately.'

The shock of what her uncle had told them left little room for thought regarding anything else and with Gabriel's sleeping arrangement as he had suggested and Laura lying wide-eyed and anxious in the bed, the night passed without any disturbances.

But not without much concern on their part for the kindly old man who had given them his house as a farewell gift when he'd gone to spend his retirement in a warmer climate, and now was having to come back to where there was someone he could depend on to provide him with the best possible treatment and care that he was going to need.

Was her uncle's illness going to be what Gabriel had needed to take him back into cancer care? It was a shame if it was. It should have been of his own free will, but at least he had promised to be there for Gordon, as she'd known he would the moment he'd been told about the other man's problem, and it was a step in the right direction.

In the middle of Sunday morning they'd seen Gordon off on the local train that would take him to a major station where he could get a connection to London, and for once Laura and Gabriel were alone. Josh was at Toby's for the day, and Sophie had been invited to lunch at the home of Lily, the school friend that she'd brought along to the party on *The Lady of the Lake*.

'Why don't we go for a walk along the lakeside and have our lunch out, just the two of us?' Gabriel suggested as the train disappeared from sight. 'We've had no chance to discuss the bombshell that Gordon dropped on us last night, although we won't know anything constructive until I get the details from the Spanish side.'

'He seemed very calm about it, didn't he?' she commented. 'We were more alarmed than he was.' She was about to say more when an incredible thought struck her.

When Gabriel had gone down the village to get the Sunday papers while she'd been making breakfast, her uncle had gone to sit in the garden and while he had been there had made a call on his mobile.

She'd thought nothing of it at the time, but on looking back she remembered that he had been speaking to someone about renting accommodation in London. Could it be that their conversation the day before had made him decide to transfer his medical arrangements from Spain to London to get Gabriel back into cancer care, knowing that he would not refuse to treat him? And now, having blithely told them he'd got an apartment in the city, was about to back it up by finding one with all speed?

Gabriel hadn't noticed her hesitation. He was wondering what the count of Gordon's prostate would be when he received it from the other hospital. It would be a good guide to the seriousness of the cancer and the urgency of the treatment required, but he could do nothing until then, and as he and Laura had some time to themselves the next few hours were going to be *their* time and no one else's.

As they strolled along by the lake he took her hand in his and when they came to age-old rocks by the water's edge that would have been there ever since nature had created a lake of such a size beneath the towering fells, they climbed up onto them and sitting side by side took in the scene before them.

'I want us to live here for ever,' Laura said dreamily. 'And our children, *and* our grandchildren.'

He was smiling. 'I would say that is pushing it a bit. In this day and age offspring want to spread their wings, and the more they see in other places the less they want to live where they were brought up. I could see Josh maybe staying put, but not Sophie. She has too much get up and go for that.'

'She was a little lost soul when you weren't around,' she told him. 'I had to keep telling her that you were looking after sick people and she would accept that for a while and then begin asking where you were all over again.'

They were actually talking like normal people, naturally, freely, without constraint, and venturing further she asked, 'How do you feel about my uncle persuading you to go back to medicine for his sake?'

He wanted to tell her that he felt fine, that what Gordon had asked of him had made his blood run warm, his brain engage, that he would do all he could to cure him, or at the least lengthen his life, but that he had wanted his return to his profession to be more in keeping with what he'd been planning for weeks and still hadn't got the go-ahead for.

'I'm easy about it,' he said, 'and if we're going to have time for lunch before we collect the children, I think we'd better make a move.'

She'd spoilt it by mentioning his work, Laura thought as they scrambled down off the rocks. Why couldn't she have kept it light?

Yet why should she have to? She wasn't the one who had made it into something not to be discussed.

But Gabriel was right about their free time together being something not to be wasted and for the next couple of hours she was how she knew he wanted her to be, smiling and relaxed, and when Gordon's name came up again in conversation as they walked back into the village to collect Josh and Sophie after they'd had a leisurely lunch, the mention of him came from Gabriel.

'I will use the London house as my base while treating Gordon,' he said, 'and liaise with the hospital from there.'

'Yes, whatever is best,' she agreed without further comment.

He was observing her questioningly but didn't say anything further. There was no point until he knew where he was up to with the rest of his working life.

That evening there was a phone call from her uncle with the address and telephone number of an apartment not far from the hospital, and Laura was even more convinced that it had been arranged *after* rather than before she had confided her anxieties to him about Gabriel's reluctance to return to his profession.

If she was right in her surmise, it would seem that Gordon had been extremely quick thinking after she'd confided in him, and had seen a way of not only getting a man he greatly admired back to where he belonged but would also be benefiting himself by being treated by one of the top cancer specialists in the UK.

He was a crafty old love, she thought when he'd gone off the line. It would be the third time he had done something very special for them over recent months. He'd given them the house, recommended her for the job, and was doing his best to bring Gabriel back to where he belonged.

Nathan had arranged to have two weeks' leave when the baby arrived and in her role of practice manager Laura was concerned about staffing problems amongst the doctors. Ruby and Hugo were fine, no holidays due there. John Gallagher had said that in a real emergency he would be prepared to lend a hand but he might be a bit rusty, and then there was Aaron Somerton, Nathan's acquaintance from way back, due to get in touch any time to give her an arrival date.

But it was all going to be rather hit and miss until the little one had actually arrived, and then it would be all systems go, with September now well under way, October ready to step into its place, and the flu-jab season would be upon them.

On the home front Gabriel had received all the necessary information he required to be able to start treating Gordon's cancer and was now in control of the situation, with the sick man visiting him each week at the town house and then proceeding to the hospital not far away if any tests were required.

He had phoned James to tell him what he was involved in with Gordon, explaining that he was treating him as a private patient and was not expecting to create any waves at the hospital himself as all test results would be sent to him by computer.

There was only one situation where he might have to go there and it was if his patient should need surgery that he, Gabriel, would want to perform. If that should occur he wouldn't hesitate, would be over the threshold in a flash with the adrenaline pumping, but he wanted it to be an orderly, organised thing if he ever went back, not a sudden appearance in Theatre like a ghost from the past.

But Gordon's count *was* high. If the radiotherapy he had arranged for him to have at the hospital didn't have the desired effect, Gabriel would be back where he belonged, performing a prostatectomy with all his bad memories and heartaches put to one side as he did what came to him as naturally as breathing.

None of that had been part of his conversation with James. It had been just a courtesy call, and his friend had listened to what he had to say and wondered how Gabriel could endure being so near yet so far away from how it used to be.

But like Laura he'd thought it was a step in the right direction and knew there was no point in them discussing him returning to any other aspects of his work until the hearing had taken place.

Gabriel had just arrived home in the early evening from his second weekly appointment at the town house with Gordon when Nathan phoned to say that Libby was in labour and he was about to take her to the maternity unit at the hospital.

Laura had answered the call and she asked, 'What about Toby? Do you want us to have him, Nathan? Josh would be delighted.'

'No,' was the reply. 'But thanks for the offer. He's staying with my father until the baby is born, but I'm sure that he'll bring Toby round to play if you ask him. You know I'll be missing for the next two weeks, Laura?'

As she was replacing the receiver Gabriel appeared and on seeing her expression asked, 'What's wrong? You look serious. That wasn't James, was it, or your uncle? I only left him a few hours ago'

She shook her head. 'No, it was Nathan.

It would seem that the baby is on the way. He's taking Laura into the maternity unit and Toby is with John Gallagher. Libby says that Grandfather Gallagher and Toby are big mates so that should work out well.'

'And so do I take it that your concerned expression is connected with staffing at the surgery?'

'Yes. It is,' she told him. 'Once we've had our meal I must get in touch with the new doctor, but first how did you find your patient?'

'Not bad. The waterworks aren't comfortable, of course. They never are in those kinds of cases, but if radiotherapy begins to have an effect soon, it might give Gordon some relief.'

The morning brought news that the Gallaghers had a daughter and a sister for Toby. The baby was to be called Elsie after Libby's mother and her arrival was the main topic of conversation at the practice, with Ruby joining in just as naturally as anyone else, with Hugo close by.

She would have had to face this sort of

situation countless times, Laura thought, and would come across it many more. When they were ready to go ahead, adoption or fostering would hopefully fill the gap in their lives.

In the middle of the morning she had a reply from Aaron Somerton regarding her enquiry of the previous night as to when he could be expected to join the practice, and the answer was that it might be three weeks due to last-minute problems at the African hospital where he was based.

Not good news with regard to staffing arrangements at this end, she thought, as now the very thing he had been coming to do was upon them, with not only Libby no longer employed there but with Nathan also away now that the baby had arrived.

It occurred to her that maybe Gabriel would be willing to fill in for a couple of hours each morning and in the afternoon before he went to pick up the children from school.

It would be far from the kind of medicine he'd been involved in, but he would have seen hundreds of patients with hundreds of problems over the years, so wasn't likely to be fazed by what he came across at the Swallowbrook Medical Practice.

The only problem was that he didn't know she was thinking along those lines, and there was his commitment to Gordon, which meant him spending a day in London each week. But four days of his presence would be better than none, and if what the doctor who would be taking Libby's place had said was correct, it would only be for three weeks that she would be asking Gabriel to help out at the practice.

There would have been no necessity to involve him if the original arrangements had been carried out, but the baby had arrived a little earlier than expected and Aaron Somerton wasn't going to be there to fill the gap yet.

CHAPTER NINE

SHE was going to mention the idea to Gabriel before she said anything to Hugo and Ruby, who were holding the fort, and his reaction to the suggestion made her feel that she'd done a wise thing in consulting him first.

When she put the question to him that evening he said, 'How do you know that the other doctors would want me to muscle in on them? I would imagine that Hugo and Ruby are very capable.'

'Yes, they are,' she agreed, 'and, no, I don't know what they will think of the idea. I wanted to suggest it to you first as staffing arrangements *are* my responsibility.'

'Don't you think the patients are going to be wary of being treated by someone with a reputation like mine?' he said quizzically. 'When I was down on the river bank the other day there were two guys fishing nearby and they kept checking that their catch was still where they'd laid it. They must have known I'd been inside and thought it was for thieving. I imagine they would have run a mile if they'd known the real reason.'

'Do you have to be so flippant about it?' she choked. 'Anyone knowing the truth of what happened would never pass judgement on you.'

'Possibly not, but the judiciary system did, if you recall.'

'Of course *I recall*,' she said indignantly. 'I can't believe you might think that I don't.'

'I'm sorry, Laura,' he said contritely, and reaching out for her he held her close. 'You are the last person I should be whingeing at. Yes, of course I'll fill in at the practice if you want me to. Just tell me what you want me to do.'

She was still in his arms and wanting to stay there, but he put her away from him gently and said, 'I've waited long enough and can wait a little longer.'

Her blood, which had been warming at the closeness of him, cooled, and as if his thoughts were already back to basics he said, 'When do you want me to start?'

'In the morning, if you will. The sooner, the better.'

'Right, I'll go straight to the surgery when I've dropped Sophie and Josh off at the school and will work through the lunch hour to make up for having to pick them up at half past three.'

'We could have lunch together in my office if you like,' she suggested.

He was smiling. 'Let's see how it goes first. If I receive a general boycott from the patients I might be back home filling the dishwasher and going around with the vac by lunchtime.'

'You are doing it again,' she protested.

'What?'

'Making it sound as if you care about the opinions of others when you don't.'

'It's true, I don't. The only person whose opinion matters is yours, and I know that it has hit a few lows over the last twelve months.'

'I've accepted all of what is past,' she told him. 'What I can't accept is that you know there are people out there who need all the help they can get and yet you are frittering your time away as if they don't exist.'

'You mean as the local layabout who is doing you out of the school walk? Are you sure those aren't the kinds of reasons why you want to get me in harness at the surgery, and has it occurred to you that your uncle might have ditched his arrangements for treatment in Spain to get me back in touch with my London roots, even though I am only too happy to do what I can for him?'

'Yes. I have to confess that it has,' she told him, 'though I wasn't sure.'

'And you didn't think to pass on your thoughts about it?'

'What would have been the point? I knew that you would want to treat him, whatever the ploy he had adopted, and with regard to me asking you to help out at the practice, it was for a few reasons. One was the shortage of staff, another was that you might enjoy the change from fishing, and I wanted us to be together during my working hours.'

'But not during the night?' he couldn't resist commenting. Even though it was the opposite of what he'd said earlier when she'd been in his arms, and he got the answer he expected.

'No, not then,' she said in a low voice, and went to call the children in from play.

Ruby and Hugo were delighted to know that Gabriel was going to fill in one of the gaps at the practice when Laura phoned to tell them later that evening, and when he put in an appearance the following morning there was none of the aversion he'd expected from the patients.

There was plenty of curiosity and quite a bit of interest in knowing that a big-wig from London in a smart suit was there to listen to what some of them had to say about their health problems and prescribe whatever medication he thought was necessary.

Hugo told him laughingly, 'They'll be coming to consult you from miles around when the news gets out that you're the new temp at the surgery. If they haven't got anything wrong with them, they'll invent something.'

Gabriel went down to Laura's office in the lunch hour and when he was framed in the doorway with sandwiches and two mugs of tea she saw that he was smiling. When she asked what sort of a morning it had been he said, 'It was better than fishing,' and for the first time in weeks she felt light-hearted.

'Why don't *you* go to meet the children?' he suggested when the lunch hour was over and he was ready to go back to the activity up above. 'That way I can work straight through until the surgery closes. I will be more help to Hugo and Ruby that way.'

She was only too happy to agree. For one thing she would get to see Sophie and Josh earlier than when she was there until the surgery closed for the night, and for another because Gabriel had slotted into the surgery type of routine as if he'd never left it, and that could only be good.

For it to be *excellent* it would have to be the same kind of thing on a much bigger scale, and how that was going to come to pass she didn't know.

As she waited for the children to come pouring out of school amongst the throng of primary and junior pupils Laura felt as if she was lit up like a beacon because bringing Gabriel into the practice, if only for a short time, had turned out to be the right thing to do, and it had been such a long time since she'd done anything that wasn't wrong where the two of them were concerned.

When Aaron had heard from the practice manager in Swallowbrook wanting to know how long it would be before he joined them there, he had been loath to inform her that he would be delayed. He was a man who when he made an arrangement liked to keep to it, but that wasn't always possible under the circumstances that prevailed at the hospital where he worked.

Two of the doctors were ill from another of the gastric bugs that always seemed to be lurking in the dry heat of the country that had been his home for the last four years, and like every other problem of that nature it was threatening to assume epidemic proportions, so he'd had no choice but to delay his arrival in the UK until he could leave with an easy conscience.

He'd been happy enough there, had achieved a sort of uneasy contentment, but from the moment he had decided to go home he had been longing for the day when he was back where he belonged, so when he'd replied to the message from Swallowbrook it had been with regret that he'd explained about the delay.

It was working well, Laura thought at the end of Gabriel's first week as locum at the practice. When Libby and Nathan called in with Toby and their newborn they were impressed to find him dealing with patients in one of the spare consulting rooms. 'This is great!' Nathan exclaimed. 'Did Gabriel need much persuading?'

'He wasn't sure if it was a good idea when I first suggested it,' she told him with the memory of his comments about the reaction of patients to his past, 'but it is working out well from everyone's point of view.' *Especially mine.*

They were having lunch together each day in her office, and she was picking the children up from school instead of having to wait until the evening to be with them, and if it wasn't exactly how she longed for Gabriel's expertise to be put to use, between them she and Gordon had found ways to re-kindle his dedication to healing.

The truth of it, if she only knew, was that they had nothing to congratulate themselves about. Gabriel's dedication to his calling was alive and well in the form of an aching void inside him that would never go away until he was back where he belonged, with those whose lives were under the threat of cancer.

Gabriel had his heart's delight family-wise in Swallowbrook and would never want to change that, but the ache inside him was stronger than it had ever been and he regretted ever telling Laura that he was going to give up medicine.

As Nathan and Libby were leaving the practice with baby Elsie, so was the patient that Gabriel had been seeing, and he came out to congratulate them on the birth of their daughter,

While Laura and Libby were chatting he managed to have a quick word with Nathan and asked him urgently, 'How much longer?'

'There is a meeting next week,' was the reply. 'You will know definitely by then, and, Gabriel, they are crazy if they don't agree to what you want.'

'Hmm,' he murmured doubtfully. 'I wish I was that sure. It's Laura's birthday the week before half-term and I do need to know before then.'

'The vicar came to see me today as soon as he heard I was helping out at the surgery,' Gabriel said when he arrived home after six o'clock that evening. 'He has had good news about the throat problem and wanted to share it with me. It would seem that the radiotherapy is working and the tumour is shrinking.'

'He is a great guy. Has had no moans or groans since he was diagnosed, just wants to get his voice back so that he can communicate with his people once more.'

There was a lift to his voice, a new purpose in his manner, and Laura prayed that it would continue. Though how could it? He was going to be working at the surgery for just three weeks if Aaron arrived when he'd said he would, and immediately after that Gabriel would be driving to London for the hearing, and if it didn't go down well, what then? Would he go back to fishing?

He'd been observing her expression and said levelly, 'Don't start crossing bridges that you don't have to, Laura. We've got used to living one day at a time, so why not keep on doing so?'

'Because that isn't how I want it to be,' she protested, 'and it isn't how you should want it to be either.'

'Sometimes we have no choice,' he told her, with the thought in mind that if the local health authority would get a move on he might be able to contradict what he'd just said and give Laura something that she really wanted for her birthday.

In the meantime, tomorrow was his day

for seeing Gordon at the town house, where he would be going over the results of tests he'd arranged for him to have over the last few days.

Blood tests and a bone scan had so far indicated that the cancer didn't appear to have spread to any other organs, which was good news, and though it was too early to expect any results from radiotherapy, he was hoping that if a full recovery wasn't possible he might at least be able to halt the spread of it and create a situation where it was kept under control for the rest of his elderly patient's life.

Gabriel was off early in the morning before any of them were up and when Laura went into the spare room and saw that the bed covers were in a tangle as if he'd had a restless night. She wondered just how much longer they would be able to endure the crazy game they were playing with their emotions and desires.

The flame was still burning, the desire just as strong, so why weren't they doing something about it?

* * *

Later that week she saw Gabriel chatting to the builder whose firm was responsible for the completion of the clinic building next to the surgery and when he joined her for lunch at midday she asked, 'Did the builder say how long it will be before the clinic will be open and working?'

'Yes, he expects it to be finished by the end of the month,' he told her. 'The guy said that there is going to be a special opening ceremony with the mayor doing the honours and all the local big-wigs present who have contributed to the cost, which I imagine has been enormous.

'I'd had a quick look around the place before you saw me talking to him and it will be fantastic when it's finished, with all the latest equipment, attractive waiting areas, a café and snack bar, and countless toilets and kitchen facilities. The environment will hopefully make patients' treatment easier to endure.'

They hadn't discussed it further as a medical rep had an appointment with her and had just arrived, but later in the afternoon she had a few moments to spare and spent them gazing across at the new building that was going to help improve cancer care in the area, while Gabriel seemed to be content to let his contribution towards it go to pot.

Baby Elsie was to be christened on the Sunday of that week with Ruby and Hugo as two of the godparents and Libby's friend Melissa from Manchester making it a total of three.

'How is the vicar going to manage that?' Gabriel said immediately when Laura told him about the christening.

'He's going to use a hand mike.'

He wasn't impressed. 'Why the rush? Some people don't have their children christened until they're walking and talking.'

'The reason is because Libby's father is coming up from Somerset for the christening. He is a sick man with severe heart problems and doesn't know how long he might have,' she explained.

'Fair enough, then,' he agreed. 'As long as the vicar doesn't over-tax his voice.'

Gabriel was on edge and knew it. He was going to tell Laura on her birthday about the holiday he'd arranged on the Greek island for the four of them, and there would be no problem about that. It was somewhere she'd always wanted to visit and all the arrangements were made.

The half-term break from school would commence a week after her birthday and he had arranged for them to fly to Greece on the Monday at the start of it. By the time they were ready to go Nathan would be back at the surgery, and hopefully Aaron would have put in an appearance, so all ends would be neatly tied up.

He intended to burden her with gifts on her special day, the holiday being the first, with others to follow, but first, before that, there was the hearing, and a phone call that he was waiting for. With regard to that he had hoped that Nathan might have some news for him at the christening.

He had, and it wasn't what he wanted to hear. The phone call was going to be delayed due to someone's illness. A meeting had been postponed and would take place the following week. So he gave his full attention to the simple yet moving service of baptism in the village church.

Later that evening when the children were asleep Laura asked, 'What was wrong at the christening? You were very sombre. Were you wishing that *we* had a tiny newborn to present for baptism?'

He laughed but it was a hollow sound. 'Our present circumstances don't exactly lend themselves to that sort of longings,' he said dryly, 'and for it to happen any other way I would have to be a contortionist.'

He was right. It had been a foolish question, she thought, turning away. Amongst the things that were not right in their marriage, *and top of the list*, was that they hadn't made love since he had been released.

She longed to lie with him and let the desire that had always been so strong between them wipe away the hurts and misunderstandings, but even that had gone all wrong. They weren't in tune any more, and until they were the future would always be a blur.

The days of the following week were dragging for Gabriel, and for Laura her pleasure at having him working in the surgery was dimmed after their downbeat conversation in the wake of the christening.

The two things should be separate, she told herself, their home life and Gabriel's career. However far apart they might have grown, nothing would diminish her delight if he ever changed his mind and went back to what he had been doing before she'd brought his neglect of her into focus.

One thing was for certain, she was expecting her birthday to be a low-key affair. He wouldn't have forgotten, but compared to years past it would have little to commend it with their lives in such a mess. She would just have to smile and make sure she didn't give away the hurt that she carried around with her all the time.

On Friday morning the phone message he'd been waiting for came through. After seeing the children to school, he called back at the house to see if there had been any calls. The phone rang while he was there and the words that came over the line were what he wanted to hear.

All that remained now was the hearing scheduled for Friday of the following week, the day before Laura's birthday. He strode out briskly towards the surgery where he was going to spend the day with the ailing folk of the lakeland valley that he'd fallen in love with. It wouldn't be the first time he'd given the sick the benefit of his expertise, and if the phone call he'd just received was anything to go by, it wouldn't be the last.

When he breezed into her office with only seconds to spare before the surgery opened its doors Laura saw that something had pleased him and was grateful for it, whatever it might be, if it was going to get Gabriel through the week in a reasonably happy frame of mind.

For her own part it was like a knife in her heart every time she thought about what lay ahead of him. The only good thing was that whatever the verdict might be from the hospital board it would give some degree of closure to the unhappiest time of their lives.

As the days went by Gabriel's good humour persisted and she began to wonder if it was due to him not being bothered either way what the verdict would be because he intended opting out of medicine no matter what, and if that should be the case it would mean that in spite of her hating the idea of him giving up, he was still going to do it.

A break in the tension came in the form of an invitation to supper at Ruby and Hugo's.

Their house, Lakes Rise, which Hugo had bought off his sister when she'd gone to live abroad, wasn't far from their own and as Laura, Gabriel and the children walked the short distance between their two houses they had to pass kennels, and as soon as Sophie and Josh saw the dogs of all shapes and sizes it was inevitable that they should want one. They were especially taken with a golden Labrador called Max.

'What do you think?' Gabriel asked Laura, and was surprised to see her shake her head. It was rare that either of them denied their young ones anything, unless they deemed it totally unsuitable, and for some reason she wasn't in favour of the idea.

So with some persuasion and a few maybes they managed to get the children to leave the dogs behind and continued on their way to Lakes Rise.

'Why don't you want the children to have a dog?' Gabriel asked Laura in a low voice, but got no reply, and as minutes later they arrived at their destination the discussion had to be shelved, and it wasn't brought up again until the children were in bed.

'If you get the all-clear from the hospital board on Friday and we have to move back to London, the city isn't the place for a dog,' she said when he asked once more what her objection was, 'And I don't want the children upset by having a pet that they can't take with them.'

He was observing her in angry astonishment. 'What makes you think we will be returning to London?' he demanded. 'Do you honestly think I would drag you all back there to fall in with my wishes? I love this place as much as you do and no way are we going to leave it because of my career, no matter what the outcome of the hearing.'

'I'm sorry,' she told him, 'but you can't blame me for thinking that one day we may have to go back to the town house in the square and the big city hospital again.'

'Not at all!' he said levelly. 'No way are we going back there to live, Laura, you have my promise on that. So maybe we can give some thought to a pet for the children in a few weeks' time.'

CHAPTER TEN

WITH a robe over her nightdress Laura was on the front step waiting to wave him off into an autumn dawn on Friday morning and he was still smiling, his good humour having returned after they'd sorted out the business of the dog. Suddenly exasperated, she said, 'I'm glad that you're so happy about all of this. Can it be that you already know the verdict of the hearing, is that why?'

'No, of course not. How could I?' he protested, and held her close for a moment. 'Are you going to wait up for me, Laura? It could be late as I intend paying your uncle a brief visit after the hearing.'

'Yes, of course I shall wait up, and will you please stop being so chirpy about today's ordeal?'

'I'll try,' he promised, and within seconds he was off, heading for the motorway and a decision that a few weeks ago he would have been dreading, but the fates had been kinder to him in the last few days than of late, and if they wouldn't let him carry on as before in London, all would not be lost.

James was waiting for him at the entrance to the boardroom when he arrived and as they shook hands his friend said formally, 'They will be ready to see you in a few moments. We are waiting for a couple of latecomers and then will commence.' In a more normal tone he added, for Gabriel's ears only, 'You know how much I want you back here, don't you, Gabriel? Have you got any plans for if you get the all-clear?'

'Er, yes,' he told him, 'but you may not want to hear them.'

'Sounds ominous,'

'Not entirely, but we aren't at that point in negotiations yet, are we?

The hearing was going as he'd expected. Some of the elderly diehards were dubious about him being allowed back, but the number of those who knew his strengths was far greater and soon Gabriel was asked to leave the room while a decision was made.

It didn't take long and when he was called back in James was smiling and soon congratulations were being showered upon him. When everything had quietened down Gabriel told him his plans and because James knew the pain and heartache that his friend and his wife had endured over recent months, he had no fault to find with what Gabriel was suggesting.

The two of them had a late lunch together and then Gabriel went to call on his elderly patient, and Laura's uncle was delighted to hear that he would once more be doing the work that he excelled in.

'Don't say anything to Laura before I get the chance to tell her myself, will you?' he asked him as he was about to set off for home.

'It is her birthday tomorrow and I'm hoping she will feel it is the best one ever when she sees and hears what I have for her.'

* * *

Laura was asleep, curled up on the sofa, when he let himself into the house at gone ten o'clock in the evening. He'd made no noise, but almost as if she sensed his presence she awoke the moment he entered the room, and as she raised herself into a sitting position the question was there. 'Gabriel! How did it go?'

'It went well,' he said softly, perching down beside her and taking her hand in his. 'I can go back to what I was doing before any time I want.'

'And do you want?' she breathed.

'Yes, I do.'

She reached up and cupped his face in her hands. 'I'm so glad, Gabriel, so very happy for you, and in spite of what you said when we were discussing a puppy for the children, if London is where you need to be, we will go back there.'

He shook his head. 'No, Laura. I meant what I said. Here in Swallowbrook is where we are going to stay. London is a fabulous city, but we are all happy here, and it would be cruel to uproot the children again.'

'So are you intending staying in the town

house during the week and coming here to us at the weekends?' she asked as the bubble began to burst, 'because if you are, it will be like taking a step backwards and I don't want that to happen.'

'No, I'm not intending anything of the sort,' he said reassuringly.

'So how, then?' she asked. 'You surely can't be thinking of commuting every day!'

'No, of course not, but there is always a way and I will find it.' He already had, he thought, and tomorrow Laura was going to know what it was.

'It's your birthday tomorrow,' he reminded her, 'and I don't want there to be any clouds in your sky, so are you going to trust me on this one?'

'Yes,' she said weakly, with the feeling that there was no way that Gabriel could combine working in London with her and the children in Swallowbrook, without the stress being worse than it had been before. Was he so much on cloud nine at being reinstated that he wasn't seeing the difficulties of what he was planning?

He was reading her mind, eager to tell

her his plans to stop her from fretting, but
her special day was only hours away, and he
said, 'Tomorrow is your birthday and there
have to be no clouds in your sky, so why
don't you pop up to bed and get your beauty
sleep while I make myself a drink, and tomorrow I'll tell you all about what went on
when I was in front of the firing squad.'

She smiled. 'It would seem that they were
out of bullets.'

'Yeah, they must have been,' he agreed,
adding as she began to climb the stairs,
'Would you like your breakfast in bed on
your birthday?'

She shook her head. 'No, Gabriel. I want
it with you and the children. I want us all
always to be together...' she raised her eyes
heavenwards '...until our young birds fly
the nest.' As she slowly climbed the stairs,
Laura thought she couldn't have explained
it much clearer than that.

The day of her birthday had dawned and
the children were beside her bed the moment she opened her eyes with the presents
and cards that they'd made, and with one

cuddling up on each side of her she opened
their childish offerings and expressed her
genuine delight at the thought that had gone
into them.

There had been no sign of Gabriel so far
and when hunger overcame excitement and
the children went downstairs she threw on
a robe and went to see where he was.

He was in the kitchen and Sophie and
Josh were eating their breakfast in front of
the television in the sitting room when she
appeared, still tousled from sleep.

'Happy birthday, Laura,' he said, kissing
her lightly on the cheek, and handed her an
envelope.

As she opened it slowly she saw that it
wasn't a card. Inside were flight tickets, a
paid-up booking form and a brochure of an
hotel beside a golden beach on an island that
she'd always wanted to visit. As he watched
her surprise become delight she said softly,
'Is this why you weren't interested when I
suggested we go abroad, Gabriel?'

'Yes, I'm afraid so.' He smiled. 'I already
had it sorted and you took me by surprise
when you came up with the suggestion, so I

had to play it down, otherwise it would have meant telling you and spoiling the surprise.'

She went up to him and held him close for a precious moment. 'How could I have thought that my birthday was going to be a non-event?' she choked.

As he looked down on to her he said, 'I have something else for you, Laura, but I want to give it to you when we're alone. Do you mind waiting?'

'No, of course not,' she said dreamily, with the thought of the holiday he had planned making her feel warm and cherished.

They'd had a lovely day, the four of them, a picnic lunch on the lakeside down by the marina, a sail in the afternoon and an early evening meal at the hotel before they went home to Swallows Barn. As Laura tucked the children in later she reminded them joyfully that they had just one more week of school and then at half-term they would be off to sun, sea and sand on a beautiful island.

When they were asleep she took off the

jeans and the top she'd worn that day and changed into a dress of soft apricot silk that Gabriel had always liked to see her in, before going downstairs to where he was waiting for her.

There was stillness all around them as she went to join him in the sitting room and when she had settled herself across from him she noticed that there were no gift-wrapped boxes or bags to be seen, and wondered what it could be that he had for her.

'You look very beautiful,' he said gravely. 'I hope that what I have for you will match the occasion.'

'What is it?' she asked with a sudden feeling of confusion.

'It is something rare and comes under the heading of "peace of mind". When I've told you what it is I hope you will understand and see it that way too.'

'What is it?' she asked again, feeling suspended in space and unable to get a footing on anything solid.

'I want you to answer me a question first,' was his reply.

'All right, then, go ahead.'

'Do you still want me to go back to on-cology?'

'You know I do, Gabriel,' she cried. 'There is nothing I want more. It was my fault that you gave it up in the first place.'

'It was not your fault and I beg you not to ever say that again,' he told her. 'Getting back to what I have to tell you, I've been asked to take over the running of the new clinic when it opens.'

Her eyes were wide with wonder. She'd been able to see the clinic as it took shape from her office window on a lower level and had imagined Gabriel finding the fulfil-ment that he was being denied there. But her thoughts hadn't gone any further than the odd moment of wishful thinking because she knew that his heart belonged to a big hospital in London, well worn, well used, that he must surely yearn to see again.

'Just like that, without any ifs and buts and whys and wherefores about your past?'

'Yes, that describes it,' he said calmly, 'but I have had Nathan on my side, deter-mined that I should get the job, and he has a lot of pull in the area's health arrangements.

'I've had a few interviews towards that end and only heard that the position was mine a few days ago. I've kept it to myself until I'd been to London because if they'd banned me I would have wanted to know if that made any difference to the job here, even though I'd been assured that it wouldn't.'

If he'd expected delight, it was slow in coming.

'But what about London and the hospital there…and James?' she cried. 'What if you grow bored with small-town medicine?'

He was smiling. 'You are incredible. I thought you would be over the moon to know that I'm going to be working in Swallowbrook. No more late nights, no more being overworked.'

'I am! Have no doubts regarding that. It will be wonderful, marvellous,' she told him with shining eyes. 'How long have you known about this?'

'I was approached some weeks ago and have caused a delay because I wanted the appointment to be on my terms and I only heard a few days ago that I had the agreement of the governing body.'

'And what are your terms?' she asked tremulously.

'That I work in London two days of every week, and for the rest am based in the clinic at Swallowbrook. I intend to spend most of my time in Theatre in both places as surgery is my main occupation, and in the case of the clinic, where there will be no facilities for it, I will do my consultations there and use those of the new hospital on the lakeside when I operate.

'I've arranged with James that I will do each Tuesday and Wednesday at his end, which will fit in with me seeing your uncle, and I will only be away from you for just the one night.

'What do you think? I hope I've got it right for everyone *and you most of all.*'

Her cheeks were wet with tears. 'You *have* got it right for everyone, and I love you so much for it, Gabriel, but is it going to be right for you? What about you?'

'I've got you, haven't I? What more do I need?' he said gently.

The tears were still flowing as he produced the box that held the eternity ring and he wiped them away gently before telling her, 'I had got this to give you on our wedding anniversary, but if you remember your job got in the way and I was introduced to the feeling of having made a meal for someone who didn't appear, as you must have done many times in the past, so the ring stayed in its box, but not any more.

'There will never be a moment that is more right to slip it on to your finger than this, but read what it says inside before I do that.' And he placed it on her open palm and waited.

'"*True love never dies*",' she said softly, holding the gold band with its circlet of diamonds up to the light, then she held out her hand and as he slipped the beautiful ring onto her finger it was as if their world had righted itself at last.

'Do you think our love got lost somewhere along the way?' he asked as he held her close.

She shook her head. 'No, Gabriel. Underneath all the misery and heartache we never stopped loving each other because ours is of the kind described in the engraving and it does last for ever.'

Lifting her into his arms, he carried her up the stairs and into the master bedroom, and when he laid her on top of the covers she gazed up at him and it was there, the need they had always created in each other. It wasn't dead, it had just been sleeping.

Later, after they had made love with passion and tenderness, like wanderers coming home after a long journey, Gabriel raised himself onto one elbow and looking down at her said softly, 'Tonight has blotted out the pains of the past, Laura, and the only thing we have to concern ourselves about now is the future, the fantastic, wonderful future.'

Reaching up, she brought his face level with hers and as their glances locked it was there in their eyes, the promise of what was to come in the days ahead, *and all of it was good.*

EPILOGUE

It was the opening day of the clinic and they were all there in the foyer. The mayor and his associates, the representatives of the area health authority, the doctors from the practice and Gabriel, looking tanned and relaxed after their Greek idyll.

Seated on the front row of chairs that had been set out to accommodate guests, Laura was remembering how he had given her the precious gift of not only what he'd described as 'peace of mind' but also a rekindling of their love.

If ever she had any doubts about that she need only take off the beautiful ring he had given her and read once again the message inside it.

'True love never dies' had been the words

of the engraving and she was wrapped around with the wonderful truth of them.

It was done. The mayor had said his piece and declared that the clinic was now open and functioning, and that refreshments were available at the back of the entrance hall.

As Laura looked around her at the immaculate newness of the place and compared it with the well-used facilities of the London hospital that Gabriel hadn't forgotten during the months of his absence, she was happy that he hadn't cast aside the old in preference of the new.

When he appeared beside her and took her hand in his it was there again, the feeling that all was right with their world and that after many long months this time it was here to stay.

* * * * *